For Sophie and Alex

ISBN 978-88-8398-071-8

Copyright ©2011 by European Press Academic Publishing
Florence, Italy

www.e-p-a-p.com
www.europeanpress.eu

Proprietà letteraria riservata
Printed in Italy, USA and UK

Alison Castelli

Visions of Venice

EUROPEAN PRESS ACADEMIC PUBLISHING
fiction *Mariposa*

Chapter 1

When I am with Valeria, I gesture in Italian, sigh in Italian, say Italian-sounding things about how the Dolomites are exquisite and the cost of living is so high. I become gentle in her sweet presence. She speaks to me with the most delectable accent from Modena, the center of the peninsula and great tortellini. I become less fearful and more hopeful. But we see each other so infrequently, like the sighting of an Alfa Romeo Junior. I'm in Italy for two months, visiting my mother's family and conducting research during my sabbatical. I've gotten tenure at a small liberal arts college on the outskirts of a quaint Pennsylvania village. I have found a life's companion and a sedentary dog, a garden, and a trusty bicycle with which to commute to the college. Yet, for some undiscovered reason (despite ten years of therapy, reading the Dalai Lama, eating better) I float sadly through life, as if there is a roof over me that prevents me from flying.

I called Valeria on a borrowed *telefonino* (cellphone). With all the traveling I do, my mother just said, "Go ahead and take mine." So I did, on the train and in the streets, sometimes receiving calls in awkward places—a restaurant, a bridge over a Venetian canal, in the driver's seat, in bed. We met six years ago after a friend said that I must. "She is a brilliant musician and an equally terrific person." So I went to Modena and jotted down an interview with her about her polyphonic choral music and life's inspirations. It was published in a grassroots women's music magazine. She told me about her macrobiotic diet, yoga and several boyfriends, all as if she were singing. She did sing often around the house, like a mouse—quietly, but audibly—so that if I was still, I could recognize the tune. She is five feet tall, with lovely straight auburn hair that her sister, she would tell me later, envied passionately. Green eyes, the color of Veronese marble, absorb the sun when it strikes them. She has tiny hands gesturing as if picking flowers in an Alpine meadow. She loves to hike and summered as a child in Champoluc in the Valle D'Aosta region of Italy—where I did too, with my mother's family. That's why I speak Italian.

Last time she told me that Italians have an incredible fear and longing for friendships with *stranieri* (foreigners). "We are going through an interesting period in history. Italians detest the new African, Asian and Eastern European immigrants. We take their money, trick them, are rude, but every once in a while one of us is open and sheds the fear of difference and helps a person in need."

"That is certainly true," I said. "I saw it myself. Last week I took the bus from Padua to Venice and witnessed this African guy getting yelled at by the bus-ticket guy. 'What is the matter with you, you stupid boy, can't you read the sign?' he said. The man got on the bus and sat behind me. Then he asked a fellow passenger how long it took the bus to get to the airport. 'That long!' the man exclaimed. 'The ticket guy told me half an hour. I have a plane to catch in forty minutes.' The Italian passenger told him to get out and take a cab. 'No, I can't. I have no money.' Then the Italian fellow called the airport on his *nino* to see what he should do if he misses his flight. 'You can get the next flight. No problem.' The African man thanked him."

Valeria had many stranger friends like me to whom she only spoke in Italian. Thank goodness. So many people try to speak to you in English in Italy these days. It's no fun.

"How are you Valeria?" I said in Italian on my phone, while driving the rented car in Padua.

There was a pause.

"I am in Italy for another month and would love to see you."

"Yes, me too." There was a longer pause. "My sister committed suicide last week. She had been unhappy for many months."

"I am so very sorry, my dear friend."

A car honked at me, and my companion, Barb, motioned me to pull over. I gestured to Barb to find a pen, and she also got me a scrap of paper. I wrote down the shocking news.

Barb whispered, "I'm sorry."

I asked her name and how old she was.

"Angela. She was forty-four, with a child and a longtime boyfriend."

I did not want to ask any more questions.

Valeria said that Angela was found in her car on the side of the road at five in the morning. A passerby noticed the car running and all the doors locked. He saw her slumped in the driver's side and a yellow rubber tube running from the exhaust pipe through a cracked right backseat window, which had been taped shut. Her purse, sweater, and phone were on the front passenger seat. He found a rock and broke open the window to pull her out on the road. It was way too late. The police, who arrived almost immediately, said she died around two a.m. The funeral, attended by many Modenese dignitaries because she was the president of the local university, happened a week later. Her father did not attend because he was devastated. Afterwards, Valeria read me a short poem about sleeping in bunk beds, talking into *le ore piccole* (the small hours) of the night—a metaphor for early morning.

Her sister went to law school and graduated best in her class, and she was madly in love with her boyfriend, the magistrate. They had a son, Giulio, who was eleven when she died. He was told that her mother had been tired and had fallen asleep at the wheel and crashed. He knew that it was suicide. Valeria said, "You could see it in his lips when he spoke." He questioned everything anyone said to him from that point on.

"Why don't you come to visit me in Venice? Please come," I insisted.

"Perhaps. I begin teaching this week. I need to prepare my lessons." She sounded concerned.

"I will be in Venice for a month. Come any time."

"I really should. My sister and I spent a lot of time there together when we were in high school."

"Good. So I will see you soon?"

"I'll call you," and the phone went dead.

I made my way back on the city street in the direction of Venice. Barb and I spoke about poor Valeria, the flower of Italy. Valeria knew about biochemistry and could read classical and medieval Latin. She had a boyfriend, whom she had been dating for three years. He had a wife and a child. Most of her boyfriends had wives. This is the fate of single Italian women. He lived in Modena and worked for the airport in Bologna. He ate a macrobiotic diet and was a great singer. He entertained me once on the piano by singing "Margherita" by Riccardo Cocciante, the Italian Tom Jones. He was short and handsome and caring and soft. But married, I thought each time we were all together.

Barb told me to watch out for green signs that directed me to the highway, the Autostrada. We had an appointment to meet Anna, the owner of the Venetian apartment I had rented. Anna had recently lost her husband in a fender-bender on a lazy Sunday afternoon, driving without seatbelts in the Veronese countryside. People die a lot more easily in Italy than in America. Maybe they have more to look forward to in the spirit life. More good art and music than we have here—not to mention the food.

The countryside just outside Venice is flat and green. Canals interrupt the farms, demarcating territories. Palladian villas sprout up in woody places. A mist hangs over the entire vista in early October, which departs only in April or on unusually cold days. Twenty-five marshy miles separate Padua from Venice. Still, we were running late and had to take the car to 160 kilometers per hour whenever possible, which wasn't very often because traffic has changed in Italy since the seventies. It used to be that guys in their Ferraris and Alfas would get into the left lane, with their hands planted on their horns, and speed by us as if they were in streaking jets. Now there is so much traffic and so many trucks that you are happy if you get to your destination without experiencing a wreck or seeing one. Trips that used to take two hours now take four. That will happen in the States too, soon.

We saw the first signs for the town of Mestre and knew we were getting close. All roads that go to Venice lead to Mestre first. It is the industrial gateway to the sinking city. It is the home of huge department stores and car dealerships, for which there is no room in Venice. Italians are compulsive shoppers. Their stores are bigger than any Sears I have ever been in. A five-kilometer jetty leads from Mestre to Venice. Built in the early part of the twentieth century, the passageway to the city is wide enough for a four-lane roadway and four or five train tracks. Old train cars full of graffiti are abandoned on this historic stretch of road. Tour buses compete to get there first. We made our way on to it and saw our first glimpse of Venice, its domes, spires, and orange- and red-painted buildings. The road gently climbed as we approached the Piazzale Roma, the last stop for cars.

Anna was waiting for us at the bus station. She did not know that we would be arriving by car. I hugged her hello, and she said to find a spot in the only parking lot. We, with my great Italian parking karma, quickly found a parking spot, and I reached in the trunk for the sheets and towels my mother had prepared for me. I also had a pair of plastic boots for the *acqua alta* (high water), which was inevitable in October. Anna pointed us to a bridge, and we immediately felt the excitement of Venice upon crossing it. Motorboats and gondolas were all around us. People with huge smiles and maps in their hands started and stopped. Anna said that I would love Venice, as soon as I got used to it. It's just different. Narrow and dirty in places. Splendid in others. She guaranteed it.

Anna said that she would show me two apartments, one big and empty and one small and quaint. We walked across steps that took us to the Grand Canal and over the blue-gray, misty water. Anna told us that her husband had died in a car accident two months ago and that she had to fight with his children and that he owned the building I would be staying in and that she knew that I would like it. He had been a film director. She said that she was destroyed and did not know where to turn. Lawyers and daughters who wanted his money surrounded her. She was his fourth wife, fairly low on the family-inheritance food chain.

Anna rounded a corner and side-stepped some dog poop on the Calle de la Laca. "This is your street," she told us. "Don't forget how to get back to your car, because I will not be coming back with you. I am taking the train to Rome." She opened the front door of an eighteenth-century building. Inside was a boat and kids' scooters. She showed me the upstairs apartment first because she thought that I would like it better. It was huge, without any furniture. The kitchen was bare, and paint was peeling off the walls. There was a musty bed in the bedroom and a dilapidated bathroom. Barb poked me gently, and I shook my head. "I think that I might get depressed living here," I said honestly to Anna. "You see, I have a tendency to be melancholy," I added apologetically.

She smiled and said, "Let me show you the other apartment."

We walked back downstairs and she unlocked a ground floor door. I walked up some high marble steps into a furnished and colorfully tiled living room space. On one side was a refurbished kitchen with a metallic stove and tiny refrigerator, tiled in bright, alternating red and brown squares. This looked better. And it had a phone and a television. The bathroom was fairly new too, and the bedroom, which faced the street, was cozy. The entire apartment was under a gorgeous dark, wood-beamed ceiling. I heard something slop outside the living room window. "What was that?"

"It's a boat. There's a canal right behind the house."

Barb thought that was wonderful. And I thought it was poetic. Water flopping up against the side of the house.

After only a few minutes, I chose the apartment we were in. Anna handed me the keys and said not to use the phone. I thought, why should I, I have a phone. She said that the apartment was mine for as long as I wanted it. I handed her a month's rent, about $600. She said "thank you" and was gone with her grief. The apartment keys were in my hand.

"I hope that I don't get too sad in this place," I said to Barb. "It's so dark and musty."

"Barb opened the living room shades, and a little light came in. "It sure is. But you will be fine."

"I hope so." I have always been terrified to be alone. Perhaps I would never see Barb again. What would I do? My mind began to spiral down its usual path.

"You'll love it here," Barb propped me back up.

We decided to go back to the car, get the rest of our luggage, and drop the car off at the Hertz in Mestre. Barb would be staying two more days before returning to her life as a lawyer back home in Pittsburgh. Her vacation was almost over. My adventure was just about to start.

Chapter 2

We spent two days with a plastic-coated map in hand. She started with a cappuccino at the local "bar," and asked the nice bartender where there was an Internet "point" so that I could use email. We needed to be connected when we were apart—with so much distance—for a month. Barb said she liked the feel of the "bar" and that I should go there with my computer and write in the mornings. I don't drink coffee. We walked across the Accademia Bridge in the direction of San Marco, passing the fashionable Versace and Gucci stores. With each step, like more water, we were surrounded by more and more tourists. The shops were empty: instead, people haggled with African men for colorful leather bags placed neatly on clean sheets. One frustrated man walked away shaking his head. There was no winning this fight. An old Venetian man yelled at one of the merchants to go back to his own country and kicked a newspaper as he mumbled. The African bid him no mind while trying to sell a fake Fendi to a blond American.

We arrived in the Piazza San Marco feeling as if we had just gotten out of a maze. The Byzantine cathedral rose in front of us, its golden domes reminding tourists of the city's Eastern heritage. Pigeons filled the square in clumps around children and older people. A pigeon sat on a five-year-old's smiling head. Kids chased pigeons. Pigeons pooped on the restored Venetian lions, and clumps of it surrounded the lampposts. Music echoed from cafés into the piazza. Jazz pianists playing American tunes worked with singers. Aggressive waiters overcharged their quizzical customers, who were paying five or six dollars each time they requested a soft drink. But who cares, this is Venice. There is a kind of tax in Venice. All the vendors add it on without paying any taxes. It is an across-the-board rip-off—twenty percent is added on to all the merchandise and services you purchase or request. Of all the cities in Italy, Venice is the one in which you get ripped off the most without really caring about it.

We walked up to the door of the cathedral and peered in. Blue-clad men with official-looking hats told us to move quickly to the right. We obeyed their commands and walked on the undulating rock in the cathedral. It felt like a magic carpet. The marble had buckled over the last seven hundred years, producing the most delightful curves upon which tourists tripped and grabbed on to their partners. The dome above us was bright gold with figures awkwardly seated in the middle. They didn't look at anyone in particular. Not even each other—probably too focused on seeing God. A little girl at a Christmas party last year asked me if I see God. She pointed to the center of the room, "because he is standing right over there." I had to know. "How tall is he?" She raised her hand above her head and said, "This much." He is small, I thought, as she jumped into my lap and showed me her silver pendant.

Barb said that she liked the mosaics and wouldn't it be great to learn how to make them. We walked to a smaller chamber on the left side of the cathedral, where an opening revealed a layer of water covering the tiles. There must have been a foot of water lapping on the stone. "I can't believe that they don't drain the water," I said, stunned. "It's going to ruin it."

"It hasn't ruined it in all this time," Barb responded with certainty. "I read that the Italians never dredge the canals. They are just overflowing." To Barb's way of thinking, that's what made the whole thing special. Venice is like a naughty child with little supervision: miraculous and unnerving. We decided that we needed a better guidebook than the one we had found in the rented apartment, which, by the way, was dirty. The bathroom and kitchen were filthy. Food was left out on the counter. The bathtub, with no shower, was grimy. "How dare they rent a place out without cleaning it first!" Barb said. Oh, right, this is Venice. My mother, the woman from Aosta, north of Turin, said that Venetians are dirty thieves. She knew this because all the nannies stole her stuff when she was a child.

We made our way to the Rialto Bridge and placed our elbows on the marble while looking down into the water. Japanese tourists filled the gondolas, and chatty gondoliers talked to one another on their routes. Water taxis rushed by them, and a noisy fireboat came by with its siren on. Wonder where it is going, I thought to myself. We talked about Valeria and how sad we felt for her and hoped that she would take advantage of my invitation to come visit. Then it was time for dinner, because time flies in Venice, especially when you are with your companion, who doesn't have another companion, which is what I happily knew at this moment. We walked back to our apartment near the Scuola di San Rocco. Should we just have a slice of pizza? No, we decided, we would have something a little better. But Venice is known for bad food. "Not if you have seafood," I said.

But who would ever eat the food that comes out of the laguna?

"People have done it for centuries," Barb said.

"But no one even swims in it," I responded. Barb and I were clearly bickering now. We had to settle the score of what had happened in the United States just before we left.

We found a suitable place to eat that seemed clean and quiet. The black-haired waiter brought us the menu instantly and took our order within a matter of minutes. Barb had the tuna salad, and I had the *fritto misto* a typical fried assortment of fish. We asked for a bottle of red wine, a Merlot because Barb didn't like white wine, and settled in to settle the score. About a month ago, we attended Barb's sister's wedding. Perhaps I need to start well before that time. We had spent the entire summer preparing for the wedding. We had seen a couple's counselor named Snickerle, who had diligently prepared us for any eventuality— except the one that happened. He said that Barb shouldn't worry about how I would act and that I shouldn't get too bent out of shape if Barb acted strangely too and that we were in this whole thing together because deep down we loved each other. Barb's mother did not like me because I wasn't Jewish and I didn't want to get married or have children. Our shrink suggested that I rent a car in Cincinnati so that I could escape if I needed to, and that Barb not get too upset if I did escape—it wasn't about her. We decided that we would get through this no matter what.

Things began well. We were housed in a fancy hotel in downtown Cincinnati. I schmoozed with Barb's enormous family. I wore an eggplant two-piece long dress and elegant shoes. We clapped after the speeches at the rehearsal dinner, and I stopped drinking after my second Bloody Mary. The next day there was a rehearsal at the park, because Amy (Barb's sister) insisted that both Barb and I be in the wedding party, even though we weren't married. Barb's mother directed each of us where to move, over and over again, as we all sweated in the Louisville humidity of a September day.

The day of the wedding I had my hair and make-up done. They put really dark make-up on me because I told the lady I was a gay professor. I would have preferred something a little less severe. She put my hair in a big ball on top of my head, with little straggles falling off the side. I pasted the strapless bra onto my body and squeezed into the control-top panty hose, gingerly, this time without ripping them, then put on my gold dress. I had refused to go to my prom, or any other dress-up occasion. The two-inch heels came on next. I looked like a transgendered sausage. Off we went to have our pictures taken in the art deco hotel lobby with a guy who once took some pictures for Jackie Kennedy. "Head, up. Turn to the left a little. Shoulders back, smile." And then all the bridesmaids had their pictures taken, and the bride. Sally, one of the maids, had lost her mother to breast cancer earlier that year. She radiated her mother's presence, as if she were with her every step of the day. I told her this as we were going to the car.

We drove to the ceremony, and I limped over to where it was all going to take place. Small talk about how good everyone looked filled the halls. The hired string quartet began the Vivaldi, and we marched to our places. I held a cream-colored bouquet of roses in my hand. A female rabbi spoke about how God made man and woman to complement each other for life. The father and mother of the bride were smiling, even though they had told us it was embarrassing to have both Barb's and my name on the rehearsal dinner invitations. All was going just fine. Until those damn pictures.

After the wedding, at the spot where the rabbi said that God made man and woman to come together, we were moved into the garden for some pre-dusk pictures. Barb's mom asked that the "family" be together for the first one. I was to stay on the side and watch. I felt embarrassed and humiliated and so I stood there and spoke to Debby, a bride's maid, about our family. Barb and I have been together for six years. We own a house together, we are on the same healthcare plan. We have a dog together. Matching towels from Sears. I figured they would include me in the next set of pictures. But no! This was for extended family, aunts, uncles and grandmas. Debby said, "This is so not right." And her mother, as a ghost, was reiterating this to me.

"That's it, I've had it." I threw the bouquet on the ground and stomped off. "No way am going to be in any more of those pictures," I said to myself, tears running down foundationed cheeks. One of the best men followed me across the lawn, but to no avail. I had made up my mind. It seemed clear that all the pretenses of family were just that. I found an isolated corner of the garden where it would be hard to find me easily. I didn't expect anyone to come running after me. I sat down on the ground and watched the poplar trees bend lazily in the hot wind. Bugs began to desire my sweaty skin. Fifteen minutes passed, and I finally got up and back onto my ugly gold pumps. Amy and Barb came to find me, and I knew I was in for a long evening.

"That was really crappy, what Mom did," Amy insisted.

"Sorry. I felt like an outcast," I immediately apologized, knowing that Barb was stuck between me and her family. Amy gave me a hug while Barb appeared as if she had seen a ghost. I apologized again, and she seemed limp. No one was supposed to confront her mother about anything.

"My mother is pretty upset," Barb finally said to me.

"I am sorry. I will apologize to her."

"That's a good idea."

We picked up the conversation in Italy at about this point. Barb asked me why I couldn't just accept her mother's behavior. Why did I have to make a scene? "Mom is unreasonable. Can't you just accept it?"

I felt my self-esteem pulled to the limits. Her mother's general dislike of me seemed like an insurmountable barrier between

Barb and me. Barb would never adore me if I didn't have her mother's love. It was hopeless. And anyway, why didn't Barb insist that I be in the family wedding picture? Why didn't her sister? What is the matter with this world?

The waiter brought us our orders. By that time I had polished off half a bottle of wine and my words began to flow a lot faster. My sentences began with "If you really loved me" and "Why don't you just?" and "This can't go on if." Barb thought that I needed to mellow out and be more understanding of the way she is. More patient and tolerant of her mother. This reasoning got completely intertwined with my sad self, which had accomplished so much (a book, a concert) but could not recognize it and felt trampled by the demands of my job. Just felt trampled by most things. By strangers, lovers, family, and the family dog, who, by the way, never gets up off her lazy ass to come to the door and greet me when I come home.

I had a hard time getting my tenure—as most women do. Despite receiving a Professor of the Year award and publishing constantly, the dean and his cronies had come up with some kind of split decision, which forced me to seek counsel and threaten a lawsuit if I wanted to stay at my quaint liberal arts college job. After hearing about the lawyer, they backed off and said that despite the fact that I possessed an "uncritical and undisciplined mind," I would be granted tenure as long as I stopped writing about contemporary women composers and stuck to my specialty, the Italian Renaissance. "Oh, Jean is not the right 'fit.'" Damn it. It is hard to fit into a straightjacket. The slightest wind in the wrong direction set my feelings of victimization into motion. Barb's mother was the breeze *du jour.*

We began to raise our voices when Barb said, "After all, it was her wedding, not yours." Ouch. I told Barb to grow up and stand up to her mother's posturing. I demanded the check from the waiter, and we found the apartment in Venetian silence. This was the last night before Barb's return to Pennsylvania. She had to get back to her job as an attorney at law. I had never been alone—without my parents or childhood friends—in Italy. I had spent every summer of my life in Italy. Spoke fluent Italian. My mother is Italian. But how could I survive in Italy without Barb? Perhaps we would never see each other again. A war could break out in Kosovo and somehow involve Israel, and then WWIII would start, and there would be no way for me to return to the good ol' U.S. of A. These thoughts were jumbling around in my head as Barb packed her bags and we quietly changed and got into bed. I hugged her tightly, knowing that we would get through this. We had loved each for at least six years, if not more in a past life.

The next morning, I grabbed the satchel for my laptop and one of Barb's bags and we made our way to the Piazzale Roma, where you catch the bus to the airport. It took us fifteen minutes to find the office to buy tickets, and when the bus came, the driver sold tickets right there to the other passengers. At least the bus is here, I thought with a sigh. You never know in Italy. Most of the time they aren't. We were surrounded by American tourists who spent their dollars with glee. One talked about the glass she bought, the other about the alabaster. I asked Barb what she thought about going back home. She said that she was looking forward to seeing our dog and friends. She didn't look forward to dealing with her mother and sister. Me neither. After checking her bags, we went to get a little tuna sandwich and cappuccino at the hotel "bar." We split the sandwich, and she said she would never be able to get something this yummy back home. I agreed as we held hands at the line to pass the metal detectors. Barb placed her knapsack on the conveyor belt. She kissed me and held me longer than usual. I watched her go through the entrance to the next hallway and walk away. It was like letting go of a balloon.

Tears gathered in my eyes as I made my way back to the bus. Now alone, I was headed to Padua to start my research. The Biblioteca Civica was my destination. It was situated near the church of Saint Anthony—the Anthony who talked to the fishes, not slept with them as some Anthonys do in Brooklyn. My bus let me off in the Prato della Valle, the biggest piazza I had seen thus far in all of Italy. It is oval in shape and had a little stream running around it and Roman statues commemorating the most famous men of Padua—Mantegna, the artist, and Livy, the historian. No chicks stood on those cement pedestals. Even though there was a very famous woman from Padua— Elena Piscopia—the first woman to get a university degree in the entire world. She never married either, and had a friend/ teacher/companion for life, who lived with her for twenty-six years and was an orphan. She had grown up in a Venetian orphanage for young musicians and played and sang in the orphan choir and orchestra. One of those orchestras was under the baton of the "Red Priest," better known as Vivaldi, the composer of the *Four Seasons.* They say that he was crazy just because all he wanted to compose were operas, and he was never very good at them.

I walked the few blocks from the piazza to the library. The *strada* (street) was filled with little women selling Saint Anthony trinkets. I saw marble, foot-high statues of Saint Anthony holding a lily, three-foot long candles with pictures of Saint Anthony on them, rosary beads, and postcards of the saint. When I bumped into one of the women, she stared at me and gave me the *malocchio* (bad eye), which made me almost want to purchase a postcard to keep the bad spirits away from me. Busloads of tourists from all over the globe came to see the tomb of the Portuguese saint. I decided to give him another look too. After all, I was writing a paper on the bronze musical angels by Donatello on the altar of the church.

I felt my life open up as if from a deep sleep. I skipped up the steps of the church and jumped in. It was huge and gaudy, with enormous arches crossing it all over the place. Saint Anthony's tomb was on the left. You could tell because that's where everyone was standing in line. Saint Anthony could heal the sick and strengthen the heart. He was known for his tongue and his extraordinary ability to preach. A black blob is housed in a gold, see-through urn: it's his tongue!

I wanted to get a feel for Saint Anthony, so I waited in line with the faithful. Some had pictures in their hands; some were weeping. We walked up to the black marble tomb and touched it. Some kissed it. I put my palm on it and tried to feel something, which I did. The marble radiated, and I shivered and pulled my hand back.

No one was standing near the Donatello altar. It looked as lonely as a parking attendant on a Sunday night. Six big bronze saints stood on top of a marble block. There were four big reliefs from stories of the life of Saint Anthony—for instance, how he opened the chest of a miser to find that there was no heart—as well as four evangelists and twelve tubby angels playing instruments. I walked around the altar several times, even though I could not get close to it because it was cordoned off by red-velvet ropes and huge pilasters. Still it was magnificent. The Madonna looked down on me with her baby in her arms, knowingly. Knowing she was destined for greatness.

I took some notes about which instruments the tubby angels were playing and turned around to look at the nave. Determined to find the tomb of Elena Piscopia, I searched in all the vestibules and on all the marble tombstones inscribed in Latin for her. Sure enough, her bust was stuck to the side of a pilaster with a dedication decreeing the triumphs of her life (her degree and great beauty and great intelligence, and how she could read Hebrew, Latin and Greek). As I had suspected, she was never married. No children, thank heavens. She was a dyke. She was certainly courageous to remain single in the seventeenth century. Maybe her mother told people that she couldn't get married because she was dedicated to learning. That's what my mother told people about me.

While strolling through the church, I got the distinct sense that people did not like me. Was it because I looked American? I wore baggy jeans and sneakers. Italian women wear tight jeans and cute, narrow shoes and gold jewelry. My hair was not combed and was gray around the edges. Italian hair is tidy, usually held back with sunglasses in some designer color. Venetian women are known for their bright red dyed hair. Italian women over thirty all have their hair dyed. No one would be caught dead looking like intellectual Susan Sontag. Not even men, really. Only when they got to be fifty-five— then they could let their hair down. Like Antonio. Gosh, I was supposed to meet Dad's friend Antonio tomorrow for lunch.

Returning to the bright sun, I squinted a little and took a peak at Donatello's equestrian statue called the *Gattamelata*. It too was covered in pigeon shit, and the proud, masculine soldier had a pigeon on his head and one on his horse's tail. He had short straight hair, which partly covered his forehead. Germany would never let a 500-year-old object decay in bird poop. Shouldn't someone move it into a museum before it corrodes and dissolves into nothing? Saint Anthony did not really notice it. It wasn't good for very much here: you couldn't touch it because it was up on a pedestal.

The library was just around the block, and I said hello to the building guard who took my bags and handed me a yellow card to fill out. I wrote on it "Prof. D'Entreves," and he took a look at my Pennsylvania ID, with a picture of me when I first moved to Pennsylvania from New York City. I looked miserably smiley. Mugging it for the camera in hopes that things weren't that bad. Wasn't I supposed to be happy? I was one of the lucky ones who got a job. My hair was messy and I had on a wrinkly collar. My face looked a bit plumper too. He said, "Grazie, Professoressa," which made me split open with glee.

I took my computer and jumped up the two flights of stairs to the reading room. Placing my laptop near an outlet was no easy task, because there were only two and one was taken. I moved a young woman's folder over and placed my computer on the wide, termite-pocked desk. The small room was filled with women. Women doing their homework, researching a family secret, writing a thesis. So here were women who looked more like me: a little disheveled, noses in books, without dye jobs. I had the number of the manuscript I needed to see and filled out another form to give to the librarian. She asked me to sign a log and told me it would be just a couple of minutes. How exciting. I would get to see the original 1430 statutes of the confraternity of Saint Anthony. This book had all the rules the monks had to follow during their days of prayers. I had seen it only on microfilm before.

"Professoressa D'Entreves?"

I signed a paper and grabbed the book from her. Covered with green and red pictures, it looked like a Christmas tree inside. I turned on my computer and began to transcribe some of the monks' rules. No dancing. Psalms were to be sung in front of the altar. I copied pages of information, forgetting that Barb was even gone, that I was alone. I jumped up to go to the bathroom, where I had to squat and pee into a hole. I washed my hands with Italian soap and went back to the computer, which by this time was flashing a warning sign that the power was low. Weird. I had only been using it for a couple of hours. I plugged it in and happily kept right on typing, until it made a squealing sound and released a puff of plastic smoke and stopped dead. Black screen, nothing. People looked at me and I pretended that nothing was wrong. I calmly returned the book to the librarian, closed up my computer and walked out into the air. "It had a meltdown. What the hell am I going to do?" I said to myself as tears started to flow down my cheeks. The first thing was to find a *carto-libreria* (stationary store), where I could buy a decent pen and notebook. Then I decided to go buy some food because there was none in Venice. I mean in my apartment.

The local COOP grocery store was full of people. It was around five on a Wednesday afternoon. Wednesday is usually my lucky day. I wanted some asiago cheese and Italian tuna fish, which for some unknown reason is so much better than American tuna. I wanted some artichoke hearts and capers. I inadvertently knocked over a bunch of celery with my plastic basket, so I bent down and put it back on the rack. As I was walking away, I saw a short old woman kick a celery stalk at me that hit my sneaker. I couldn't believe it. Then she walked over to the grocery store lady and began telling her what I had done, pointing and shouting at me. I guess she did not think that I understood or spoke any Italian, so she gave the lady an earful about what I slob I was. I proceeded to tell her that it was an accident and that she had some nerve kicking celery at me and that she just didn't like Americans or any *stranieri* and should be ashamed of herself. She just shook her head and stamped off, incredulous and disgusted by my irreverent response. I felt humiliated and alone. Alone and sorry for myself. So what's new?

I paid the cashier, who also snobbed me by not even looking me in the eye when she took my money, and marched my yummy groceries back to the bus station with my broken and expensive new computer. I plopped myself in my seat and stared out the window as a symphony of cellphones went off. The air outside was hazy, but the bus driver navigated the stubborn traffic gracefully. I opened the new notebook and began with "I'm not sure where to begin. Perhaps at the major fight I just had in the store. I should get back to the apartment and regroup. Calm down. So I am back to paper and pen—like I began. Perhaps in these weeks I can learn to be a better person. I certainly mishandled the wedding photo stuff. I want to be a stronger and more compassionate person. Thank you, diary, for this solace during this time." I looked up and smiled at the man next to me. I could already feel a change coming over me. From beyond me.

Chapter 3

The next day I set out for the Marciana Library, which is located in the Palazzo Ducale. "I need to go to the library near San Marco, under one of the archways," I said out loud. How magnificent. *Nino* in one pocket and a book bag of pens and paper, I left without my foldout map, only to find myself right back at home after fifteen minutes of following a few signs for Rialto Bridge and Piazzale Roma. I got all twisted around in the labyrinths of *piazze* and landmarks, a copy shop, the Internet café, pigeons drinking at a fountain in the middle of a *piazza*. I never felt so good being so lost. It didn't matter; I was witnessing a miracle of gray canals and colorful boats, of school children with bright pink knapsacks and little black and white dogs sitting in store doorways. I felt in my pocket for the keys and unlocked the door. There, on the desk, was my map. The phone rang and I reached for my jacket pocket.

"Pronto."

"This is Antonio. Are you still free for lunch today? I want to introduce you to my friend Lisa."

"Yes." I hesitated for only a short time. "Yes, I would love to meet her."

"Where will you be?"

"At the Marciana."

"Good. We'll meet you there at one. Is that OK?"
"Perfect. It gives me a couple of hours to work in the library. By the way, do you know anything about where I can get my computer fixed?"

"No, sorry. Perhaps my son knows something. I'll ask."

"Thank you. See you later."

Map in hand, I made a left this time and passed the church of Saint John the Evangelist, then a left again over the bridge that crossed the canal called Rio di San Stinto and came upon the glorious Church of Santa Maria Gloriosa dei Frari. I had to stop and see it—this was part of my research. Otherwise I might as well be in Allentown. I paid the woman sitting in the booth six euros and she smirked at my Italian. I walked in and saw the most incredible sight: the fifteenth-century wooden choir stalls. They towered above the tourists in all their mosaic beauty. I say mosaic because each stall consisted of millions of tiny pieces of wood fitted together to make pictures of angels, saints, and luscious landscapes. A tourist pushed me as I stood before it. An old man began speaking to me in a Venetian accent and filled me in on the history of the place, saying he was a native Venetian and knew her history inside and out. He had studied it after retiring from his job in the textile industry.

I made my way to the tomb of Claudio Monteverdi, who flourished in the seventeenth century. It was simple and had some red and white carnations thrown on it. He was a fabulous composer of opera specializing in music for heaven. I mean for the angels to sing up there. He was their favorite composer. Next I moved to an altarpiece by Tintoretto. Mary was standing by the cross with some other saints and a man who was looking directly out at me. I looked at him carefully, and he looked back knowingly. He smiled. I smiled back. Had others seen what I saw? I took a great big breath and stood still and watched as a shadow drifted away from the picture and into the church. This was the first vision I had seen in Italy—and I felt queasy.

I had seen spirits in Pennsylvania the year before. The first one was in a cemetery. It was an old man standing near a tree. He waited for me to bike up the hill and told me not to worry about school and its politics and how they had almost denied me tenure and were marginalizing me and treating me like a jerk. Then he sent a squirrel darting off in front of my wheels, and I came to understand what was important, as I stopped pedaling to avoid the little fella. But as I resumed my trek and got closer to the old man, he merged with the tree and became a breeze. I looked hard and harder. He was gone. I spent the next several months looking for him—not seeing him but seeing others, more and more, among the trees. They came to greet me, never scaring me. Just taking my mind off my intense feelings of inadequacy. The college's actions only served to magnify my own emptiness and lack of self worth. You see, I had everything now and felt, while riding down the steep hill, like taking my hands off the handlebars and drifting off the side of the road to stop the pain. I had been really close to taking medication. I was desperate.

I had been going to therapy on and off for ten years. I knew the causes of my frustrations, the lack of familial support for my choices in life—my parents' not being able to come to grips with the fact that I was different and did everything my way. They criticized me tirelessly about clothes, men, career choices. Their obsessions and fears trickled into my blood like a transfusion. I had suffered and drank too much and had bad girlfriends. My androgynous attitude made me ripe for ridicule and unwanted attention. But the hardest feeling to compute was the one that I felt every day: I wanted my life to end. Days were too long.

During the last therapy sessions before my trip to Italy, I told my beloved shrink about the spirits, and she thought that *that* was kind of different. I asked her if she thought I was sick in the head—and she said no. She just listened, as good shrinks do. And said that I had really progressed from the day she first worked with me, some eight years ago. I asked her why I still felt like shit. And she said that she didn't know, but that she was sorry. I always felt better after talking to her for an hour, but like any compliment, hers was as if it had never been uttered. Instead my mind was cluttered with what professor so-and-so said about me in my tenure file: I was an uncritical and undisciplined person. And what my mother said when I screwed up the Brahms Waltz during my recital: I was a selfish and egotistical person at age 11 and I needed to put my fears of performing aside and think about the music. These words pinched all day long like an annoying little sister. In Italian the word is *stuzzicare*—prod with something sharp. A toothpick is called a *stuzzicadenti*. My obsessive self-doubt was like a *stuzzicadenti* in my heart, puncturing it and leaving me flat. The college could never have hurt me that much if I hadn't been mushy enough to let it.

I saw another vivid ghost in Oregon—in the woods. I was mountain biking with friends. I was tagging along at a slower tempo, avoiding rocks, and keeping my hands firmly on the brakes while descending a path, when I saw her. A woman in her forties with a big smile looked me directly in the eye and startled me. Did my friends see my reaction? She didn't say anything—just smiled and disappeared. She was wearing a green turtleneck and black pants, and did not look like anyone I ever saw or knew. I told the shrink about her too. I told Barb and a few friends. They picked it off like a piece of lint on a black sweater. No big deal, they all thought—it's just Jean.

I quickly checked my watch and realized that I'd better get going or I would miss having any time at the library. As soon as I stepped out of the church, my phone rang, and I thanked God that it hadn't gone off in the church, where red signs proclaimed that they were off limits. It was my cousin Chiara, calling to see if I was OK. She is so sweet. I have treated her shabbily over the years, never giving her credit for anything much. She is a married biology teacher in the local Italian school. But she had been reaching out to me—lately. We went hiking together in Gressoney. She told me her problem with her brother's girlfriend: she was an ungrateful and pushy person. Chiara was harassed by my aunt and uncle because she refused to make lunch and dinner every night for her husband, the doctor. They thought he was going to leave her for this. Couldn't they see that there was more to her than cooking! I finally did. She was indeed a special person.

She asked my how life was in Venice and if I felt lonely. I said no, following the yellow signs for San Marco. She asked me if Barb got off OK, and I said yes, and thought, isn't she sweet. I said we'd talk again soon (I am so abrupt about ending phone conversations) and continued my route across the Rio Foscari (home of the University of Venice). Then I came upon the huge, rectangular Campo di S. Margherita. All the piazzas (except for San Marco) are called *campi* in Venice because they were originally grassy areas where livestock grazed. Now they are covered with marble—undulating slabs punctured by a few trees. I crossed the length of the campo and looked up to find yellow arrows directing me to San Marco. There were two: one pointing one way and the other exactly the opposite way. Someone, a prankster, had added arrows, making the sign completely unclear—like Bugs Bunny at an intersection in Albuquerque.

I opened up my foldout map again and decided to cross the Rio San Barnaba and take a left at the Calle del Traghetto. *Calle* in Venetian means street, and *guai* (phooey) if you say *strada* (street) by mistake to a Venetian. I became distracted, once again. This time by an unusual storefront window. I never look at windows, as I do not enjoy shopping for new things— and I don't make a lot of money and will not in the future because I went to the president of my ccollege to say that a student of mine had come to my office to tell me that his newly appointed dean and right-hand man, Al Fondler, watched pornography on the Internet while talking to her. The president asked me when the student had complained and I said last month, but that the alleged event had happened a year ago. The president said that it was after the one-year statute of limitations on this stuff. No big deal. I was sickened by the whole thing and knew there would be no more raises for me.

I stopped dead in my tracks and began starring at my reflections, ten, twenty reflections. The window was full of convex mirrors, in all sizes and with different colored wooden frames. Do you have Van Eyck's *Arnolfini Wedding* painting in mind? It's a dazzling image of a man holding a woman's hand: behind them is a convex mirror that captures their backs, the easel, and the painter. That picture moves me to the core. I love the mirror and the little gray terrier that stands in front of the couple. You can see these mirrors in banks and at corners with narrow driveways. I looked at a small one and read the price tag of 100 euros. Others with more elaborate frames went for twice as much. The shop had a beagle at the door, and inside was a mess of round mirrors, some on the walls and some displayed on tables. An older woman was squabbling with her son, while a patient American looked on. The *calle* I was on proceeded to dead end into the Canal Grande, and as soon as I noticed my error, I shook my head and turned around past the mirror store and stopped again, mesmerized. But I moved on.

The Church of San Barnaba had an exposition of eighteenth-century glass sculpture. I walked in and noticed that it would cost me ten euros and walked out. This would be for another day. I made my way to the Calle della Toletta, which made me snicker because it sounds like "toilet." A bookstore inhabited one of the corners, so I took a quick peek at the window and walked in. I wanted to know if they might by any chance have the book I wrote on women in Italian music that was published by an Italian press. I asked the guy politely where the music books were, and he rudely pointed to a section without stopping to look up at me. The music section was tiny, and I wondered why people stopped buying books about the great composers and opera. Wasn't it good stuff, those stories about Mozart dying of a brain injury and Wagner marrying Liszt's daughter Cosima? My book was not to be found, even though the store did have a couple of Italian titles by my publisher. Being a feminist in Italy was like being a bird watcher in New York City. The birds are there, but you don't see them around much.

I walked out and did not say *arrivederci* or anything mildly friendly. He didn't like me because I looked American. That seemed to be the standard treatment Barb and I were receiving in Venice. After the toilet, I crossed the Rio di San Gervaso and ambled over to the Gallerie dell'Accademia. A huge building housed this most famous art gallery in Venice, facing the Accademia Bridge, a wooden structure that crossed the Grand Canal. In addition to the permanent collection, Giovanni Bellini's restored paintings were currently grouped together on display.

Bellini is the Leonardo da Vinci of Venetian art. Not that I know very much about him, and that was another reason why I was in Venice, to get to know. Bellini painted a ton of Madonnas, which aren't the worst things, since at least they were women. I was curious to see the show, but it would have to wait for another day. No, I could make it. I still had an hour and a half before I needed to meet Antonio. So I wouldn't

get to the library today. Big deal. I was in Venice, not Ann
Arbor or Cambridge, Massachusetts. I had no remorse—I had
tenure and I deserved not to work for a little while. What with
the agony they put me through last year, those mean, women-
hating, lesbian-baiting bastards.

I got in line to pay for my ticket and handed my jacket and
bag to the checker. Two short Venetian ladies with bright red
hair cut in front of me, and I got up enough nerve to mention
that fact to them. They shook their heads in disgust and said,
"She is obviously not European!" Was I snobbed! Can't they
see that I am half Italian? My mother is Italian. I speak Italian.
I am half European. I replayed that scene over and over in my
head for the first half an hour of wandering in the exhibit of
gold and red paintings done on wood. Why couldn't I just let
this kind of thing go? What is the matter with me? All those
years of therapy and I still let something so minor get me so
down? I am a spoiled brat. What would Barb have said back
to them? American tourists crowded the exhibit with annoying
questions and regurgitations of their college art history classes.
Mobs of German tourists with tidy tour guides stood pensively
in front of pictures. My mother told me there were better
tourists in Italy this time of year. I wonder what she meant—
but I know she was right. People had fancier shoes on and nice
umbrellas. Whatever. I was coming apart at the seams now.
Floating through the gallery.

I made my way through the permanent collection of Italian art
to the rooms that housed the Bellini paintings. The exhibit was
called *Puro Bellini* (Pure Bellini). All the paintings had gone
through major restoration—they had been cleaned and painted
over and were bright like shiny shoes. Madonnas who had once
worn the dark frown of distraught mothers now looked like
Madonna, the "Material Girl." Somehow I think they got the

two women mixed up. Wasn't it all about material anyway? A Swiss bank underwrote the whole operation. That' s when my phone rang. Shoot. These people are going to hate me. I grabbed it off my belt loop, while a crabby guard told me to speak in the hallway, away from the paintings.

"Pronto."

"Jean?"

I was thrilled. "Miriam?"

"Yes, darling. I am zo glad you called. Zorry zat it took me zo long to get back to you. I am zorry zat I did not get to zee Barb." She spoke Italian with a slight German accent.

"She is sorry, too. She will just have to come back to Italy very soon. How are things?"

"Fine. I have been taking care of my mutter. She is getting veaker. She's having trouble getting out of bed."

"I am sorry to hear that."

"Vhy don't you come down to Florence zometime?"

"I'd love to. Do you, by any chance, have a computer I can use? Mine has died. I have to write this paper for a conference in Toronto next month."

"I have two."

"Great. Does one have a printer?"

"Yes, ze one out in Porciano does. Let's spend time out zere so I can be vizi my mother."

"Sounds great."

"I'm busy zis veekend, but vhy don't you come down ze next?"

"OK. I'll call you later next week. Thanks Miriam. Love you."

"You too."

Miriam is better known as the Good Witch of Porciano, a friend of the family who worked as an accountant by day and as a spiritual healer by night. My father introduced her to me when I was starting graduate school at Columbia in music. He thought I needed some free advice, since he assured me that no matter how much I liked musicology, it would be difficult for me to get a job.

She hung up. I felt better. With a big smile, I walked around the exhibit in a circle, until I came to Bellini's *Allegories*. There were four of them painted on small wooden panels—they were once attached to a dressing table. An image of a woman holding a convex mirror immediately caught my eye. She was standing on a circular marble slab surrounded by three angels holding instruments. She was naked and pointing to a red-clothed male figure reflected in the mirror. I moved closer to the image to read that it was called *Allegoria della Prudenza* (Allegory of Prudence) What did it mean? The figure in the mirror must be the artist, but why are there musical angels involved? Whatever it all meant, I felt deep in my gut that I had found the topic for the next article I would have to write. The connection between music and the mirror was too rich to let pass. It was like my thesis in graduate school about music and fresco painting of the fourteenth century. Music and something else—was all I ever wanted to study. It was like parmesan cheese on something else. Parmesan on tortellini, Parmesan on gnocchi, Parmesan on minestrone. How could you go wrong? I was drawn to this for the thrill of the connection, not for any real intellectual reason. During my tenure battle, the dean said that I was too untraditional within my own field of feminist studies. Too interdisciplinary. Not focused. Not serious. Not disciplined. I listened to every word of what he said as if spoken from God. I crumbled under her pressure. I remembered my shitty grades in college.

I think that I explored my self-hating nature in *Cauliflower*

Head, my first novel. (This is my third; the second has become *Fiammetta*.) My shrink in Pennsylvania says I am self-hating because I discovered I was gay when I was young and my family did not accept it. She should know all my problems by now. I've been with her for six years. I was so whiney. So pathetic when we first started working together. My hair is really long now. It looks like a daphne plant, not a cauliflower. We started because when I arrived at Mead College, my period went crazy. I was getting it every other week—and heavy. I made an appointment with a gynecologist in our small central Pennsylvania town. She had big breasts, which she covered with a tight red, fluted turtleneck. I never really understood why she had to lean over me to do a breast exam but I felt her nipple touch my mouth at one point. After my examination, she had an hour session with me in her office telling me that I was fine—just a nervous wreck. Who wouldn't have been after that examination? Instead of medicine, she prescribed a shrink. I've gotten rid of the bad girlfriend syndrome. I've got a loving person now. My period is regular. But I am still so depressed. Tenure. Dog. Dead inside. Frightened.

I took another look at the curly-haired image in the mirror. It shined and snarled. Prudence looked anything but with her big belly, long legs and long hair. A German tourist bumped into me and said "Zorry." I smiled. No problem—it was time for me to go. I had half an hour before I was to meet Antonio. I retrieved my bag and began climbing the Accademia Bridge for piazza San Marco. Men with easels lined the bridge, painting the view of the Grand Canal to the west. One painted like Monet, all diffuse, the other like Poussin, all serious and realistic. Both were really into it—you could tell from their smiles. One day I would stick my easel on that bridge and draw. Drawing was on the next horizon for my starving artistic voice.

The majestic church of S. Maria della Salute rose in the distance, and in the foreground you could see Palazzo Loredan and Palazzo Balbi Valier. Most of these grand edifices were abandoned—too expensive to maintain. Water rushed into the first floors, slopping up onto the stucco facades. Venice was crumbling before my eyes, and weary and rich dreamers replastered its beauty constantly. Black gondolas floated like wild rice in a Christmas stew. Japanese tourists snapped pictures. I saw a gondola with a sad woman and a man on his cellphone. It reminded me of the Christmas tree I saw in a metal trashcan on Seventh Avenue in New York on December 23.

I made my way to the Campo Santo Stefano, which was also huge, and known for the music conservatory that it housed. Well-dressed young musicians with their instruments ran to their lessons. My phone rang.

It was Valeria.

"Hello, Valeria!"

"Good to speak to you."

"How are you feeling?"

"Not so well. I feel afraid."

"What is it?"

"My sister is tormenting me in my dreams."

"What is she doing?"

"She is slapping me on the head."

"What do you do?"

"Apologize."

I kept following the signs for San Marco and sidestepping tourists, who were growing in numbers.

"Why don't you come up on Friday? We can spend the weekend together."

"I can't this weekend. Cesare and I are going to his country house." I told her that the following weekend was not good for me, and she said that she would come to stay with me in two weeks. "Sounds great," I told her, and said goodbye. "Poor thing," I said to no one in particular.

My time was running short when I came upon the arcade of the Piazza San Marco. Pigeons filled the air as tourists rushed to get another ice cream. I was to meet Antonio at the door of the Marciana, and I was running a couple of minutes late. Cheesy jazz streamed out of the cafés as I rounded the corner at the Palazzo Ducale. I saw a man standing with his foot up on a wooden plank laid out for floods. He had bright, long silver hair and a blue wool jacket draped over his shoulder. He saw me coming and waved. Dad must have given him a clear description of me: bushy hair pulled back into a ponytail. He gave me a kiss on each cheek and said that we were waiting for his friend Lisa to join us too. Lisa sold sweaters, he told me. She owned three stores and rented out a perfume shop in Padua. I will like her, he said. No doubt.

Antonio was insecure, like all of my dad's friends. He told me that he thought my dad was the greatest person for coming to Padua and fighting the bureaucrats, getting them to stop destroying an old library that housed Renaissance manuscripts in their attempt to improve city traffic. Italian traffic changes all the time. Streets that were once one way in one direction are suddenly one way in the opposite direction. "Those jerks in City Hall sure listened to him. They had to. He has so much power." Dad teaches comparative literature at Columbia University, my alma mater.

Listening to people go on and on about how great my dad is still brings a sickening feeling into my soul, despite the fact that I am thirty-nine years old. My anger and impatience with him as a dad has slowly melted into acceptance and respect, mostly because he began to treat me better. He really supported me during my tenure battle two years ago. He said that he would sell his house in Tuscany to pay for my lawyer bills—you've got to love a dad who says that. Even if he was a homophobe when I first came out in 1981. He said that I was a good for nothing, lazy loser. I bet he wishes that he never said that.

Antonio was short and skinny and had sparkling blue eyes. While waiting for Lisa, who is always late, he told me that he was a retired airline pilot for Alitalia, the Italian national airline. He flew jumbo jets all over the world for thirty years. He told me that Boeing models were much harder to fly than the McDonnell-Douglas. Women are so friendly to me, he continued. People in general. They put their lives in my hands and I am a kind of savior to them. Then he told me that he has three children, two boys and a girl. The boys live abroad and the girl in Rome, but she never speaks to him and they haven't seen each other in three years, since his divorce from his wife Sara, who doesn't speak to him either. Then I started to understand why: he talks all the time. His daughter is practically homeless and writes him only when she needs more money, which he is eager to give. He drives down from his villa outside Venice to Rome once a month to deliver some furniture and money to his mother-in-law, who knows how to get the stuff to his daughter. Poor guy, I thought. That was another quality in my father's friends. Many of them were despised by their families. The daughter should go easier on him. Even if he doesn't listen.

He told me that he bought a villa outside the town of Feltre some ten years ago. It was built in the eighteenth century and has three thousand square meters of space. He owns ten geese, one of which his old girlfriend *La sciagurata,* the person who dumped him, gave him. He was in love with her, a beautiful artist who paints on velvet. She was world famous for her art. But for some unknown reason, she dumped him and told him never to call her again. He obeyed like a gentleman, even though he did continue to call her names. "Maybe you can meet her one day. You would like her very much. But I can't see her. She won't let me."

Antonio's son was coming to visit him that weekend from London, and he asked, "Why don't you come and spend the weekend, too?" I told him that I would get back to him, and he said to decide soon so he can prepare my bed. I would sleep in his daughter's room. It's beautiful and has a fireplace. A villa in Italy sounded like a good adventure for the weekend—but I did not know Antonio enough to know whether he would ever take me back to Venice. Maybe he was a weird guy who kidnapped women in his villa. Wait a minute, my parent's' friends might be jerks, but they weren't criminals. I calmed myself down a little and continued to listen to him.

He told me about the history of the Marciana Library and the Palazzo Ducale. He said that he had been to several concerts of Renaissance music in the San Marco church. He loved Monteverdi and Gesualdo and told me when they were born, as if I didn't know. I nodded a lot and interjected a quick comment about the Beethoven concert I had seen in Philadelphia the month before. It was like talking to the pigeons. He just kept on pecking, moving his head up and down with each word.

The time was passing slowly as I listened to story after story from a renowned rambling professor. Soon I realized that I must stop listening or I will lose my mind. But as soon as I did, he asked me a question about what he had just said. "How would you handle my daughter?" Or "Have you ever flown to Alaska?" He became frustrated when I hesitated in my responses. He continued on about his days in the military in the seaside city of Rimini, and how he couldn't keep the women away from him.

Finally Lisa appeared, dressed in the highest of fashion, though she was of small stature. She was wearing purple alligator cowboy boots with two-inch heals, a purple shawl and black pants. Her complexion was dark and her hair was black. She apologized for being late in a whiney, sing-songy voice as entrancing as her slightly odd look. She gave Antonio a kiss on each cheek and pulled out her phone. "I have to call Amanda. Listen Amanda, make sure you put those shirts I just picked up on display. Si, sì. No problem. I will call you later," and then she gave me her fullest attention. She spoke Italian with a strong Paduan accent, which was nasal and closed. She said my Italian was excellent—putting me at ease right away. The only thing she could have said that would have made me even more relaxed was that I should wear my hair down because it is so pretty. She would accomplish this in a week or so. She suggested her favorite restaurant in Venice, *La Vedova* (The Widow). Lisa was not married, but she was not a widow either. She was, together with Valeria and Miriam, one of the few unmarried women I knew in Italy. And unlike Valeria and Miriam, she cared about money and had plenty of it. She was an entrepreneur with many rich boyfriends. Antonio had managed to get that information to me at one point.

We made our way toward the Rialto Bridge, stopping to look in the windows of Coin, a chain store found all over Italy. Cohen had become Coin over the centuries in Venice, Antonio told me. He knew everything about everything, which wasn't too bad when he was acting as tour guide. We walked on the busy Calle dei Fabbri. Many streets in Venice were named for occupations like *fabbro* (blacksmith) and *orefici* (jewelers). The *Vedova* restaurant was just off to the right of the busy street, and after a quick cigarette, Lisa walked in, as if she owned the place. The patrons at the bar said hello, and they led her to what must have been her favorite table. She ordered us a bottle of sparkling white wine from the region and asked me if I had eaten typical Venetian food before. No. So she ordered white fish salad, and baby octopus, and little fish cakes. Each delicacy tasted like one, and I ate each bit with delight.

Antonio began talking about the crooked and stupid mayor of his town of Feltre, who is sidestepping zoning laws and allowing a condo to be built along the southern outskirts of his property. It will permanently change his view of the mountains. He talked of the dead goose he found at his doorstep one night. "They are just trying to scare me. They can't. I will fight them until I am dead." No wonder Dad and he are best friends. They liked to fight bureaucracies. He began talking again of his ex-girlfriend *La sciagurata*, who was one of Lisa's best friends. She had set them up. What was she thinking? I thought. Then he told Lisa of his still-broken heart. Lisa had since found *La sciagurata* another boyfriend. "Get over her, Antonio. It's over. Move on with your life." To which point he dramatically emoted, "I can't. She broke me."

Why do some men say "broke" when talking about women? My friend Marny told me that our Mead College president said to her on a date that he wanted to break her. How romantic.

Lisa then accused Antonio of being a *noisoso* (crying bore) and told him to get a life. He smiled and said that he had to go to the bathroom. She turned to me. "Listen, I want you to meet Susanna—she's *La sciagurata*. You'll really like her. You seem like a nice, sensitive girl. She will like you too."

Lisa was saying all the right things as I drank more wine and began eyeing the plate of breaded, deep-fried little fishes placed in front of me—*fritto misto*, a specialty of Venice. Each crunchy bite was so delicious. I usually don't like to eat things that were once alive, especially if they were once swimming around the Venetian lagoons. But a little fish wasn't the worst thing for my low iron levels. I had become a "vegetarian" the year before after a bizarre encounter with a dog at Logan Airport in Boston. Waiting for my flight, I saw a forty-pound dog caged in a doggy flight carrier. It was whimpering and the kids were crying as they were waiting in line to check it in. That did it. I never ate another piece of chicken, pork or red meat after that—which was no easy task, since I loved salami, and pork chops, and grew up on veal cutlets (after all, I am half Italian). Mom freaked out incredulously when I told her to please find me some tofu next time she was at the market in Florence. I no longer wanted to be a person who ate a living thing. I still eat fish, though, on occasion.

Antonio began talking about the Tintoretto frescoes at the Scuola Grande di San Rocco. "It's his Sistine Chapel." Not may people know about it. I shouldn't miss it. Lisa grabbed his arm and said, "Isn't he wonderful. He knows so many things." Antonio, charmed by her compliment, talked more and more, until he looked down at his watch and said that he had go because he had an appointment up in Feltre with his lawyer. Lisa and I looked relieved as he paid for lunch and ran off. "Jean, I'll call you later. Perhaps you can come up to the villa this weekend." He was gone.

Lisa pulled out her cellphone and told me she was going to call Susanna. "You have to meet her. You are a sensitive person." How did she know? For all I knew of myself, I was a hard-nosed New York academic kid, born of a tough, rude father and a brilliant, self-involved mother. My mother told me my whole life that I was too sensitive. So I became hard like the skin of a potato. How dare Lisa say that I am sensitive? Twice.

Susanna was in her studio and invited us over for tea at

around five. She said that Hemmat and Dalu were staying with her and did we mind. Lisa said Susanna is a worldly person, has traveled to Asia and Africa, but not to the United States. She has millions of friends—a wonderful achievement, one I wanted to master. But how? How do you get more friends? I tried and tried at work. Barb and I hosted lovely dinner parties for my colleagues, but they never invited us over. Maybe I am so caught up in my own pain, my own past mess, that I appear unavailable and distant. Aloof and opinionated. I look in the mirror and don't see anyone. Just a reflection. But many opinionated people have lots of friends. Look at my parents. The phone never stops ringing at their home. Lisa had friends. Barb had friends. But like the ocean, mine seemed to recess from the beach to oblivion. What the hell am I thinking? I grabbed another butter cookie and a swig of Vinsanto. A good thing about Italy is that you can start drinking at two in afternoon and not worry about a thing. No one seems to work.

Lisa said that Antonio was completely delusional about Susanna. She felt sorry for the guy, nothing more. Susanna never wanted to marry him. Sure she visited his villa, but never alone. Lisa was always with her. They did lots of things together. Susanna had lost her parents young, and her brother was an ungrateful wreck who received a monthly check from his successful sister and never said a word. Lisa had a similar type of brother. "He is a bastard," she told me, "an artist who beats his own mother and his wife. He never had a *lira*. I even went to therapy to try and deal with him. But he is a violent and disgusting person." I asked her if she thought Antonio was dangerous. "No, not at all." Did he ever stalk Susanna? "No, no. He is a victim and needs her to come to him. Underneath it all he is still a gentle person. A nice, and in his own way, a caring person." Would you ever go stay in his villa? "Not alone. But it might be kind of fun if his son is there. It is a beautiful place."

We got up and made our way to Coin because Lisa wanted some new shoes. She also purchased a set of candles and a scarf. "I don't need any of this crap," she said after gathering all the packages. I followed her like a daughter in a department store, in a kind of Italian heaven, steeped in the culture and scents of Italy—but for the first time away from my own mother, who was embarrassed by my masculine body and masculine tendencies. Lisa thought I was sensitive—and not in a bad way. "I am sensitive," I repeated in my head as she brought me to a café and ordered coffee and more wine. That was the problem with my life: I need more wine and less introspection. More wine and less therapy, more wine and less worrying. My *nino* rang and I excused myself from the table and went out into the street. Lisa smiled as I got up. It was Barb, and for the first time in a decade, I heard ecstasy in my own voice. "Lisa and I are in a bar. She's a friend of Antonio. He's gone. How are you? I miss you so. Only four more weeks until I see you again. The dog? Good. Fat? Oh. Work? I see. Thanks. I'll call you soon as I can. Love you. Love you."

Lisa was busy flirting with the Arab waiter when I returned and excused myself. She began with compliments. "I knew I would like you from Antonio's description. He told me about Donatello's angels and your job." She paused, "You are a great woman." What? God had given me a new friend. Thank you, God. "I have always wanted to go to New York. Yes, I will come visit you. Maybe around Christmas. That is OK with you?"

Why does she like me so? Maybe I am just a nicer person in Italian—maybe I am more myself. She told me about her beauty stores and her mother, who she was desperately trying to get away from her crazed brother. She has a twin, who looks nothing like her and is tall. I said that I have a very successful and handsome brother, whom I am sure she would really like. I felt like San Pellegrino mineral water in a bottle, all ready to spray out. I wanted to dance and live and sing and thank God. The wine felt good.

Susanna's apartment on the Calle Groppi was filled with *objets* that she had gathered on her trips abroad. Huge wooden horses stood on Persian carpets, and plants decorated the high-ceilinged living room. She lived on the ground floor, and a green courtyard reminded me that Venice was built on turf, not only on marble. A tubby white cat sat on her dining room table as we walked in, interrupting a conversation that I heard end with "this is Giotto's daughter." Lisa walked me into the room, while Susanna was on the phone dealing with a distraught business partner. "Make yourselves at home," she gestured, "I'll be right there."

The old, white-haired woman who had made the Giotto comment was the first I said hello to. She knew the truth. My father is famous, someone people appreciate for his strength and wit, his unconventional style, his interest in other women despite the fact that he is married. Dad's career has really taken off. He won the prestigious Glinker prize for excellence in literary criticism for his book *Giotto Before Shakespeare*, describing the relationship between the master's paintings and Shakespeare's sonnets, a discovery Dad had made one day while sitting on the john perusing a Giotto picture book. His reputation preceded me with this group of straight women, and I sat down next to Hemmat, who said she was from Egypt.

The one who had blown my cover said that she was Dalu, and lived in Paris and Rome. She had command of the evening from the start. She said the music of Monteverdi was magnificent, the painting of Schnabel abominable, and shrinks wretched. I felt myself automatically get piping hot even though I should have just kept quiet, as I should have done at Barb's sister's wedding. That whole episode was still coloring my time, like a fog, even after Barb had left. I felt guilty or stupid or simply underappreciated. I could have been a nice medical doctor for all Barb's mother cared. I said aloud that I had been to a shrink for ten years and counting.

"Poor thing," said Dalu. "You must stop this immediately. It's a crutch. They use you for money. Why should they have the privilege of listening to all your stories and still get paid? It is by nature an unequal partnership, an immediate bad marriage."

"No," I replied, my voice rising in volume. "My shrink has helped me with my family. Pointed me in the right direction. Comforted me during trying times."

"My point exactly," interjected the crafty Dalu, who in the next breath would tell me that she taught design in London when she wasn't living in Paris. And that when she was a girl, one of her boyfriends had dumped her, which had depressed her and forced her to see a shrink, who told her that she needed to nurture her feminine side. "What dreadful advice," said Lisa. Right on, thought I. Dalu kept talking about the damage done by her dreadful shrink, the makeup worn and the gowns tossed to the floor. The whole time I could only think "crutch." Was Dalu correct? Was Dr. Janet a ten-year crutch? She loved me more than anyone I knew, and helped me see that I was an artist too. Not only a sort of drippy academic, but capable of writing. I always was a writer, from when I was a child, poems and little stories and the diary that my mother read every morning while I was at school. Writing kept me alive in high school. Writing took care of my feelings when they weren't being heard. Writing held memories that could be used and embellished upon like a favorite pair of jeans. Writing housed my philosophy of life, which I was slowly evolving. Jean's philosophy of being. Would anyone care?

My current philosophy of life ran something like this: We are born into painful circumstances, which we repress in different ways in our childhood. Some people become cheerleaders to be part of the group, some bury themselves in music or writing in a lonely attempt to find companionship. There appears to be no middle ground in childhood. Debacles and delights. College, if one is pushed to go, is particularly painful, because sex starts then. Sex means a general confusion about what the hell love is. I could love someone in an evening. It would have to last forever. That's what we said. Then, the post-college missteps, too much drinking, an STD perhaps, bad lovers, a fallout with parents, and then someone suggests a shrink and you come to understand that you are going down the wrong path, because you are not sympathetic to your own needs, and you act out because you think that you are a shit head. That's what your parents have always said.

The first two years of therapy you spend convincing yourself that your feelings have meaning and need to be expressed and the hell with everyone if they don't understand. I dug up stories about how my dad had a girlfriend and basically ignored us kids and how mom was so controlling and said I was ugly and a disappointment to her because I did not like to shop or do girlie things. My therapist was the only person who could feel my pain and told me to feel it all the time. "Don't be afraid, dear." I loved her for this. For listening to my silly stories. For telling me that I was getting better even when I still felt suicidal. For the compliments. Soon I hated my parents to the core because they had denied me the childhood I deserved. I despised my mom because she was so embarrassed by me. I knew that she was right somehow—because she was so smart and so intuitive about everything. Is your mother gifted that way? Most are, and they remind us of it at every occasion. She never would accept that I am a lesbian—I always was, and always will be.

Therapy then moves us to the step of forgiving our parents for being such impossibly selfish people. This may take years. I forgave my mamma for telling me that I would never amount to anything. I forgave my father for his nasty temper and arrogance. I even begin to forgive myself for being a crabby and impatient basketball player, and telling my coach to take Elvira Sacchi out of the game when she had three turnovers in a row.

I began to spend more time with my folks, stopped missing Christmases and sent birthday cards. I stood up to my sexist department chair, and asked him to consider diversity when making the next hire in the music department. Yet after all the therapy, the hours of talking about how my college had almost ruined my career—thank God for a good lawyer—the lovely relationship I was building with Barb, I felt bleak. Over the years I must have spent $20,000 for shrinks. Like a recent investor in the high tech industry, I was now empty, my philosophy of life in tatters. The journey I had confidently begun was stalled on the turnpike, without a cellphone or other lifeline. Where to move next?

Dalu rambled on about her former husband, about how he left her for a younger woman. With drama and her white hair swirling about her head, she mouthed the words "Damn him." Then she continued: "Not that I haven't had my share of experiences. My lovers in Paris during the seventies. 'Davide' was magnificent—his curly hair—" She paused. "But there were many."

Susanna asked me if I would like some tea and cookies,

and I nodded and asked if I could help. Her kitchen was built into a blue and white ceramic-tiled wall. Each centimeter of potentially empty space was covered with a photograph or a plant. She had several of herself in her twenties. She was a dark, sensuous, curly-haired beauty, with green eyes and a curvy figure, presently in black, tight jeans and a dark brown wool sweater.

Susanna introduced me to her third guest at the table, who had slipped back into the group from a longish stint in the john. Hemmat from a town some two hours south of Cairo. She had large brown eyes, which protruded from her face beneath short, dark eyelashes. Hemmat and Susanna had met near the pyramids, by chance. Susanna had driven up in a white Lincoln Continental, and everyone sitting at the local café waited to see who would walk out: it was Dalu and Susanna behind big brown sunglasses. Susanna got out to ask Hemmat where she could find a good hotel, and their friendship began.

(I notice as I write that I cannot listen to music and write at the same time. When I am truly in the writing groove, silence breathes in my mind, a blank slate. When I listen to music, I can do nothing else. Deep listening, as Pauline Oliveros might say, is what making music really is. Music is writing—that's why you can't do them at the same time. This idea will make more sense as my story unfolds.)

Hemmat smoked skinny cigarettes as she spoke shaky English. She smiled a lot and nodded after she completed a sentence, and it was difficult to understand a word, let alone tell her that I didn't. I laughed and said yes when Susanna asked me if I would like a glass of prosecco. This is Italy. They asked me why my Italian was so good. "My mother is Italian—I grew up speaking Italian."

"That's why she is different from other Americans," I heard

Dalu whisper to Susanna. It was only now that I begin to see the advantages of having been raised in two cultures. Until now it just seemed like a huge burden. I missed Italy when I lived in the U.S. and vice-versa. No one liked me really to the core in the United States, and I looked like an outsider in Italy, and I did make a few grammatical errors in my speech. I had suppressed my love for Italy in the last five years because I found Italy barbaric. The country did side with Hitler during the war. For southerners, the hatred of northerners seemed as natural as the sun. I said this to the table. "What of the racism in Italy?" They said that I had some nerve to speak after what the U.S. is still doing and did do to blacks. "But we are conscious on some level that our behavior is disgusting and needs to stop. Many Italians publicly express their prejudicial views, without hesitation." They listened. And I listened to myself carefully as well, to make sure that I was making sense.

I had struggled with race all my life. Wanting to do the right thing, recognizing the struggles that African-Americans endure every day. I finally resolved that the best I could do was get myself out into the community. Meet folks different from myself. I had pushed the president of Mead to encourage diversity on campus. (It is not hard to do. We have one black full-time member on the faculty.) In a June meeting I told him that the college was not doing enough to promote a more ethnically and racially diverse campus, which would benefit our students. He hit me with "It's a quality issue, Jean, not quantity. We would hire diverse faculty if good ones were out there." This response made me queasy for two days. Race and ethnic diversity were not a concern for this administrator, content with keeping his big-business board content.

Susanna offered up some of her delicious fish fry, fresh from the market. "I will show you where to buy fish whenever you want." The evening continued in much the same manner, as Dalu pontificated about art while Susanna looked at her as a grateful orphan of a sexist society. I was drunk and full of ideas, feeling that I should probably stop relying so heavily on my shrink. Dalu was right. I thanked my guests and accompanied Lisa to the train station. The moon was bright on the water as we crossed into the Jewish ghetto.

Chapter 4

It was Friday evening, five-thirty. I walked across the Ponte degli Scalzi, a steep bridge over the Grand Canal, climbing into the sky. Trying to save some money, people schlep luggage duffels and rollies over its marble steps. Africans sell leather belts and purses, and Asian women set up radios, selling little metal Mickey Mouse figures that appear to be dancing suspended, to disco music. Children sell little wooden train sets. I climb through the clumps of people, whose energy resounds, each surviving in whatever way feasible. Humanity in all classes and colors claimed this bridge, a microcosm of heaven.

Why I was waxing spiritually these days is part of a change I've been sensing in the last month. And I am not talking about "the change," menopause, though sometimes I wonder. Could God exist? Those of you who were raised as atheists might particularly perk up your ears here. God has been non-existent because I couldn't sense her presence. If something was beautiful, a flower, a jump shot, a skyscraper, I couldn't feel it. Its beauty was visual like an acid trip. When I was a child I felt life so deeply that I got sick. "Sick with the flu" would be the impact of climbing a tree and experiencing the flood of its energy. "Dizzy spell" was the result of jumping up and down on a soft, grassy, wet plot of land and rolling down hills and running back up until I couldn't move. "Stomach aches" from loving the taste of homemade mayonnaise my friend Marilena made in Champoluc so much that I spread it on five eggs. Mom told me to stop or I would eventually get sick and die.

Most probably I would get some kind of cancer because cancer hits people who aren't stable, like you, she said. She hadn't seen a child so sensitive. "If you don't stop being so sensitive you are going to die." I spent days in bed with mysterious ailments: a sore neck, an aching head around my temples—mind you, at the age of eight. Too much needle pointing. I began needle pointing at seven after my Aunt Magda, a mean, big-jowled seamstress, who was my grandma's sister, gave me some yarn and a pattern for Jewish Christmas. Jewish Christmas just meant that my Jewish family got together on Christmas Day to eat yummy Italian food my mother prepared, and not to think about God. She gave me a small pillow cover to needle point, with the head of a gray and white poodle on it. While watching television with my family—we watched a lot, *Mission Impossible*, *The Ed Sullivan Show*, *Laugh-In*—I needle pointed. I needle pointed wallet covers and eyeglass cases. Needlepoint is a little like paint-by-number or completing those puzzles where you search for words horizontally, vertically, diagonally and backwards. It makes an active mind passive. It puts an ocean back into a river. So does TV.

My ocean into a river happened in other ways, too, like my piano lessons. Mrs. Mirna Safranski was my teacher. She was my mother when the real one couldn't be bothered by a birthday party or cake. She was my mother when the real one drank too much wine while Dad was with a girlfriend. I loved her, but she made me play piano like a river. I was told to play only the notes on the page in only the correct rhythm. A note out of place meant a scolding and stopping, the equivalent of stopping every ten feet when riding a bicycle. A bicycle—now that was true freedom. Pedaling as fast as possible, flying over bumps. Up these steps to heaven I walked on my way to the Stazione Santa Lucia. Heaven definitely had steps and flat places where you could ride your bicycle.

At the top of the Ponte degli Scalzi, I hung my head over the water. Gondolas zigzagged, garbage bobbed, it was magical. Bounding back down to earth, I took a left at the bottom of the bridge and saw stacks of *panini* (sandwiches) behind musty glass. Hand-painted signs read "5 euros" and stacks of Cokes read "4 euros." Converted into dollars that equaled around $4.25, which does not seem exorbitant. A coke on Disney World property will cost you a lot more. Still, I'd learned after buying two Cokes at a sidewalk café for fourteen euros, and sending the café's owner and waitress to *a quel paese* (hell), that there was a tax, not a state one, but getting ripped off in Venice was an across-the-board phenomenon. Who cares, since you are in Venice?!

The Santa Lucia Station is one of many in Italy built during fascist times. The dead give-away is the flat roof and marble or cement architecture. These stations still stand all over Italy—Alessandria, Montecatini—with a certain haute couture style. A series of marble steps leads to the main atrium, forcing weary travelers to once again lift heavy bags crammed with souvenirs. I smiled remembering some American college students on their post-baccalaureate tour of Europe.

My train for Treviso was leaving at six and I still had to purchase a ticket. Treviso is a wealthy town some twenty-five miles northwest of Venice.

Purchasing a train ticket in a major Italian city is as pleasurable as driving out of New York City on a Friday afternoon: no matter how much time you leave you should have left more. My nerves were starting to feel frayed and, when I saw the confusing neon headings above each ticket seller and the double lines of customers, they got worse. Should I stand in the line that says *treni nazionali e internazionali* or *treni nazionali*?

Or *regionali*? I chose *nazionali* and waited behind a group of kids with backpacks. They wanted to go to Florence, Rome, Milan, Paris. By the end of their list, the ticket guy sent them to another line. I spoke to him in my Italian while wearing an American outfit. So he treated me poorly.

"Treviso, *andata e ritorno*," I said meekly.

"What?" he responded rudely in English.

"Treviso, *andata e ritorno*."

Not looking at me, he took my twenty euros and while chatting with his friend handed me the ticket and my change.

"*Grazie*." I felt the familiar pain of rejection. I took the ticket and checked the departure times on the board. I ran to the newspaper stand to get a *Herald Tribune* because I like to do the crossword puzzle and read the sports page. Spinning thoughts whirl around in my head that I never do very well on the puzzle because I'm not smart like my girlfriend Barb or my Aunt Becki. How debilitating they are, these thoughts. Sometimes a cloud envelops my soul and feels like a big hamburger on my heart. Here is a good question on a heart exam:

Does depression feel like:

◊ Dancing in water
◊ Sitting in mud
◊ Talking to Mamma

I find beauty in such multiple-choice questions, as long as they do not count for anything.

I made my way to track eight. The brown- and green-painted Italian train was covered with graffiti that looked as if it were imported from Brooklyn. It said Mario and *Viva I Gay* (long live gay people), and *Viva la Lega* (long live the northern separatist party). I found a seat in the non-smoking car facing forward so I wouldn't get a stomachache: it was a little commuter train without the usual romantic cabins that seated six. I pulled out my journal and began to write a few lines about how lonely I was feeling, when an American family sat down. They were three generations, and Grandma and her granddaughter sat across from me. They obviously loved each other very much and said very little. The daughter asked me in Italian if I was Italian and I said yes. I was proud that she thought that I was. We waited and chatted for ten minutes, until the train finally left the station, crawling down the tracks. It came to a dead stop some half a mile onto the isthmus. We waited and chatted, and Italian high school kids talked on their *ninos*. There was a sudden jolt and the train began to move backwards. The German tourists sitting next to me looked more forlorn than usual in Italy. I found my *nino* to call Antonio and tell him I would be late, I was going back to the station with no warning from the conductor, but Antonio did not answer.

We chugged back into the Santa Lucia Station in Venice and came to a stop. The doors were opened, and we waited with no indication from anyone about what was to happen next. I smiled with delight: this was Italian confusion at its most delectable. I continued to make some headway with the crossword puzzle. The American family turned out to be a military one, stationed at Aviano Airforce Base. Grandma told me that she was born again, and that she dedicated everything to her God. Come to think of it, she did have that look in her eye—as if she just knew better than me about what is right in the world. As if she saw something I didn't see, a kind of spiritual chip on her shoulder. She said that she and her husband were in Europe for a month, traveling on trains with a Eurail Pass. They had been to ten countries in three weeks, standing sometimes in crowded train hallways. They loved Norway best because it was the cleanest and most beautiful of all the countries. Italy was a mess. The military parents kept excusing their little daughter for nagging me. She is a little touched in the head they said—which is why she liked me, I thought. I am good with mavericks.

After fifteen minutes of just standing in the station, the train took off again for its destination of Treviso. The Italian kids made a joke about how the engineer finally figured out which engine on the train he should be driving. They laughed and I laughed and translated my laughter to the American family. Seems as if the least the American military could do for their soldiers abroad was to teach them the language, especially in Italy. Mestre came and went as did some other minor towns until I got off in Treviso, walked down the steps under the tracks and began looking for Antonio, hoping he had not left and gone back home to his villa.

He was there, not pissed off, and walked me to his car. He asked if it was all right if we made a few stops first. I was a little hungry, and if the stops involved something to eat, I would be very obliging. First we needed to pick up an engraved set of spoons he had left at a jeweler's. They were for his son and his son's wife. He told me to wait in the car at an illegal parking spot because there was nothing else. "These Trevisian cops fancy themselves German," he said. "They give tickets for everything. Sit in the car and if one comes, speak to them in English. They won't bother you." So I did—I waited.

He came back quickly and showed me the beautiful silverware that his mother had left him. Antonio can be quite thoughtful, when he isn't talking. But then he began. He told me how they changed all the traffic directions in Treviso: Roads that once went west, now go east. Roads that once went both ways, now go one. This was all in an effort to diminish car traffic in the *centro*, or town center. Instead it made people curse bloody murder because it meant that they had to navigate all around the city in order to get anywhere. Antonio got to a street and started cursing because it went the wrong way. I watched as he drove really slowly and cut other cars off without signaling and came to abrupt stops to check out a store window and lost his way and cursed and pulled over to ask directions and forgot what the guy said and went down the wrong way on one-way streets because he thought that was how it should be—all the while talking to me about Treviso's Roman heritage.

Then I remembered that he used to fly 747s around the world.

We finally made it out of Treviso and in the direction of Feltre, a town tucked in the shadows of the Dolomites. He said that we would make two stops: one to visit his friends Anna and Mario, and the other to visit Carla and Paolo. Anna and Paolo had been married for ten years, but now each owned a villa and had a new partner, which began to sound like a Neil Simon play. They would love to meet me, especially since I was the daughter of his famous friend, and I remembered my nickname, *figlia di Giotto*. My identity was wrapped up in my father's with Antonio. He wanted to impress me to impress my father. Whatever. My lonely soul needed company this weekend.

Antonio started telling about his life in the army and how—and I don't know why—he doesn't have any problem with homosexuals. He said that when he was at a party in Rome, the famous artist John somebody swaggered up to him as he was gazing at a painting and said that he was handsome and wondered if they could get a drink later. "You have such an unusual look," the artist said, and Antonio continued smiling. Antonio was not interested in him in "that" way and even felt a little flattered. He said that homosexuals were strange people, even though he has nothing against them. All they want to do is have sex. They love art and beautiful things.

This conversation made me a little queasy, especially since I am gay and in the closet in Italy. I had spent a lot of my time at Mead College talking to faculty and students about the need to create a safe academic environment for all our students. So I told Antonio that not all gay people love art, and gay people are in all walks of life, and we need to accept people for who they are, not stereotype people. He said that was fine and proceeded to announce that people from Treviso were especially known for being greedy. We continued our trip along the windy and rain-drenched Alpine roads, stopping abruptly so Antonio could show me a villa designed by Palladio. It was flooded with lights and looked like a yellow flower on a dark canvas. "It's miraculous, isn't it?"

I craned my neck to get a glimpse of it, while Antonio told me that Palladio's real name was something else and that his father had tried to dissuade him from becoming an architect, even though his teachers said that he showed early promise. Palladio studied Roman architecture and blended that with contemporary Renaissance aesthetics. Blah, blah, blah. When I tried to make a comparison between Renaissance architecture and music, he did not listen and went straight on to a point about Palladio's other villas in the region. This made me sick. I stopped listening and sank into my own thoughts about the rain and his terrible driving.

Antonio pulled the car over near a big metal gate. We had reached Anna's villa in Asolo, the home of Robert and Elizabeth Browning and other erudites. He rang the doorbell, and the automated metal gates opened for us to enter. A gravel road led to an enormous cement structure, and Antonio pulled the car to the right alongside a shed. A tidy dachshund came running through an open door, barking. Italians really go for purebred dogs. I rarely see mutts in Italy. In fact, at this moment, I can't think of any. A platinum-and-gray-haired woman came out to give Antonio a big hug.

"Anna," he said leading me through the kitchen door, "this is Jean D'Entreves, daughter of the maestro." She led me into an enormous sitting room with nineteenth-century oil paintings on the wall. A fire was lit and her husband was opening a bottle of white wine. A bowl of peanuts was on the table. Her husband was a professor of film at the Foscari University in Venice. He seemed previously married, by his easygoing manner. I asked him about the Anna Magnani movie that I had seen on television the night before. He said he never saw it, and I immediately thought him a phony. Magnani is my favorite actress. He was a phony academic, I thought, who used his professorship to snare a wealthy Venetian aristocrat.

Valeria had told me that Italian academics fancy themselves on the left of the political spectrum, often condemning the United States and championing the remains of the Soviet Empire. She said that no matter what, when they hear that I am American, they will make a comment about how barbaric the country is because of the death penalty. Sure enough, Mario sat back in his chair as if notifying an awards committee of an award he just received, and asked me how it was that a country as "civilized" as the United States could be so medieval. He followed that up with a comment about what *bauli* (trunks) American are. "Trunks" is slang in Italian for fat people. "They are enormous. I see them on the streets in Venice, hauling their huge asses from store to store." I retorted that not all Americans were fat, and that many people in my country were starving and living with very little—until I realized that was despicable. I was in a corner. We were fat and greedy. He noted that fact and I asked Anna where the bathroom was so I could wash my hands. She led me behind a gorgeous kitchen to the help's bathroom.

Brass knobs and towel hangers decorated the room. She had opted for striped blue-and-white wallpaper and a blue toilet seat. I locked the door and looked at myself in the mirror. I had stopped picking the blemishes on my face since I was in Venice, and began to notice that my skin was looking much better. I began to realize that it was a nervous habit—and had to stop in Venice because the lighting in my rented bathroom was so poor I couldn't see what I was picking. Perhaps it was also because I was eating better, less processed food, no potato chips and fewer Cokes. The prosecco was going to my head, and I smiled at the mirror, did not touch my face, and sat down. I wondered how long I could keep that up. I peed slowly and deliberately, thinking of the rain and Anna Magnani. I tried not to get down on myself or think about missing Barb and my dog.

Back in the living room, Antonio was filling in Anna and Mario about his latest escapades in the town of Feltre. Someone had stolen one of his geese, the one *La sciagurata* had given him. Yesterday he had five geese, today only four.

"Perhaps a dog ate it," said Anna.

"No, they can get away from dogs."

"Perhaps it flew away," I suggested.

"No, they have nowhere to go."

"Perhaps it will come back," Mario tried to console him.

"No, it is gone."

Speaking to Antonio was like speaking to oneself. He didn't really listen. Once his mind was made up, it was locked in for good.

Anna was stone cold, at least to me. She must have sensed that I was not normal, asking me if I had a boyfriend, and I cavalierly said yes, without any explanation. She has a daughter who got married at twenty-three and has a baby and lives with her because her husband took off. I thought that it was nice that Anna was so generous. She had that true Venetian accent that almost sounds Spanish. They pronounce Venezia like "Venecia," very nasally. She reminded me that she was from the Veneto region on both sides of her family and that her mother's side was aristocrat from Pordenone and as a child they used to play in her grandmother's castle's stables.

"And what are these paintings about?" I asked, pointing to the eight canvases on the wall.

"They commemorate the glory of the Habsburg court."

"Are you related to them?" This was the family that employed Mozart in Vienna.

"No, they were friends of the family."

I was clearly outclassed and she would not let me forget it.

Antonio looked at his watch and said that it was time to go to our next appointment with Paolo and Carla at their villa. We agreed to see each other on Sunday to go to an art exhibit in an eighteenth-century villa near Udine.

"*Arrivederci*," I said.

Antonio jumped back in the car saying what a lazy and incompetent guy Mario was. "He does nothing all day long. That book he is doing on Veneto architecture in film is a farce. He has been trying to finish it for twenty years." I told Antonio that Mario gave me bad vibes. He said why, and I said that it just felt that way to me. I did most things based on instinct, including writing my dissertation. It was about time that I embrace that quality in myself.

Antonio continued to ramble about Mario and then moved on to the story of Anna and Paolo's failed marriage, since we were going to meet him and his new wife next. Like most aristocrats in Italy, Paolo met Anna when they were young. They had sex, children and, finally, got a divorce. Antonio said that even though Paolo had a lot of money, he was a weak man. He ran his father's glass business. He and Anna were never a good match, since she wanted more from life than he, and doesn't that make for a bad combination. I listened, thinking that "marriage" is so weird. Barb and I had been together for six years and treated each other with respect, never tired of one another and never cheated. Marriage seemed too complicated.

As I write this novel I realize that you may be thinking, why am I reading this? I am floating in a sea of details and people's lives. I am here to interrupt the narrative to say that this is what life is all about. I will defend my position to the end: I write what I feel. By the end you will know why.

Antonio pulled into Paolo's driveway, a virtual construction site. His new wife Carla, an architect from New York, had left a million-dollar-a-year job for Paolo and Italy. She was Carla Mainardi, a famous, fashionable designer-architect, with a degree from Harvard School of Design, only forty-five, and according to Antonio, still gorgeous.   Paolo came running out in the rain to meet us in the driveway with umbrellas. "Come here, old man," he said to Antonio, forever kidding. Why do men talk that way? In backhanded terms of endearment? Antonio introduced me as "Giotto's daughter," and they led me up some marble stairs to the main living room. Carla, a star, greeted me at the top of the stairs. She was dressed in designer clothing, as if she had just been at the Oscars party, and kissed me on both cheeks.

"Welcome," she said in a bizarre accent. Was it from Brooklyn, London, Los Angeles?

I thanked her and she showed me her new sitting room, which she had just designed. She was redoing the whole place herself. You could tell it was designed by an architect, so sparse, so square, so full of windows. On the table were fresh chunks of Parmesan cheese and full fluted glasses of bubbly prosecco wine. She sat down and spoke in a booming voice, all charisma.

"We are living like squatters," she said about all the construction. Then she showed me the new bath they could finally use, with a Jacuzzi, two pedestal sinks and fluffy towels. "We just began using it this morning." She told me that the wood was imported from Ecuador and the tile from Tuscany. The velvet wall hangings were from Venice. "You know Antonio's friend *La sciagurata*?" she asked with a chuckle. "I bought them from her." She said that she wasn't quite happy with the toilet, which was French. More satisfaction was to be found in the mirror, which was Italian, from Venice. "Have you met *La sciagurata*?" I said that I had, without more detail. I did not want Antonio to ask more questions.

I sensed that Carla had done much more with her life than I will ever do. She had class and education and lots of money. She was well known and was flying to London in the morning to complete a business deal. Her hair was as dark as Coke, her eyes as green as *crème de mente*. Her skin was swimming in moisturizers, her body covered in a dark-blue Armani pants suit, and a cashmere sweater caressed her neck. She wasn't still asking her parents for money to go on vacation. She had obviously struggled to get what she had now and never questioned it. She earned it.

I told her I was a professor of music in Pennsylvania, and she responded as if she had seen a nice trinket in an antique store. How quaint. Women who wanted to shake up the world were not teaching music in a small liberal arts college. Women who wanted to be famous were not following in their father's academic footsteps. They were busy out there being entrepreneurs, actresses, Gloria Steinem. Not being depressed, like the half-baked poppy seed cake that I was. A walking glop of yeast. I drank two or three glasses of prosecco and compared myself to Carla for fifteen minutes. Then I told her that I was a writer—I had penned my first novel, *Cauliflower Head.*

"Really."

"It's my dream come true."

"I would like to do that some day."

"You would?"

"My job is not as creative as I want it to be. I am quitting in a couple of weeks. Paolo is giving me a room downstairs to be my studio. I want to paint."

So I gave her my speech about following her dreams. "Never take no for an answer. People told me that I could never play soccer and play the piano. And look at me: I'm a music professor. Whoopee." I said it sarcastically, because I, at the age of thirty-nine, still did not know what the hell to do with my life. "But I shouldn't be giving you counsel. You are clearly already a star." She dressed and spoke and considered life as if she had been flying in first class when she wasn't even on a plane. "Excuse me, Carla. I did not mean to be condescending. I am sure you know how to get things done."

She showed me the master bedroom. It was black. Black bed, black paintings, black down comforter. A big mirror stood behind the bed. "It's still not quite what I want. It needs a dresser. I am considering a chrome dresser to match the mirror." She had a set of chrome boxes in the corner. "I like to store my books in there." While Carla appeared warm, her decorating was not. She said that her family still lived in Boston and that she had no brothers or sisters. "Did you like Anna?" she asked as we walked back to the men.

"I thought she was nice, but a little chilly."

"That's been my impression too."

"Do you spend much time with her?"

"No, I only met her at a wedding. A friend of Antonio's."

I wanted to tell her that I liked her much more, but thought better of it. I would have fallen in love with Carla too if I weren't in love with Barb. And the prosecco enhanced these feelings. Carla was Carla—if you know what I mean. She was very shapely and sexy, which didn't hurt either.

Antonio was busy telling Paolo what a jerk Mario is. What a stupid. What an imbecile. He knows nothing about film. "Have you ever met anyone so stupid? I don't understand what she sees in him." He paused.

"He seems faithful," Paolo said.

"That cannot be enough in life," Antonio responded. "He is insipid."

We listened to them speak. I began to feel nauseous from the combination of cheese and wine. We hadn't had any dinner and it was ten thirty. Antonio said that we were going to eat at home with his son. "What time?" I asked.

"They'll be there around eleven. We should probably go."

We said *arrivederci* (until next time) to people I might never meet again, except in a dream, where a lot of my one-time acquaintances find lodging. They waved at us in the rain, and Paolo communicated one last manly insult to Antonio, who said something like "smell you later" in Italian.

Antonio drove into the rainy night, slowly and deliberately, like a pilot trying to park the plane at Kennedy Airport. He chatted about his ex-wife, who lives in Vicenza, and his son and daughter-in-law, who both work for the same British bank. British banks are taking over the world, and no one is doing anything to stop them. The French are mad at McDonald's. They are directing their ire at the wrong enemy. Can you really conquer the world with hamburgers? You can with money.

The British are ancient sore losers, still stung by the American Revolution. Remember they own pharmaceutical companies and are media moguls. I pondered these things as Antonio described a sexy encounter he had at the symphony a couple of years back. "She couldn't keep her hands off me," he said.

We passed through the town of Belluno on our way to Feltre. It could have been Newark, for all I could see through the rain. I was using up a lot of energy trying to keep Antonio's ideas from penetrating me. He began talking about Mozart and Beethoven, and I thought that I could contribute, but as soon as I said something like "Mozart had a very talented sister named Nannerl," he said so did Mendelssohn and Mendelssohn's grandfather was a rabbi and Mahler was Jewish. I took in a big balloon of air and sighed deeply. "How much longer?"

"Only ten minutes," he said and went back to his music history lesson, which was particularly appalling, since he knew I taught music at my small sexist college. We finally entered the town of Feltre, and we followed the brown signs for the Villa Taddeo. A tall cement gate introduced a long driveway. The windshield wipers were on maximum speed when Antonio jumped out of the car and flipped on the lights. Miraculously in front of us, we saw a gravel road with statues on each side. The bumpy road led to a huge boxy building, and Antonio pulled up his car next to another large, more rectangular structure adjacent to it. We got out and Antonio said that he would get my bag from the trunk.

"This is my villa," he said with pride.

"No one else wanted it."

I looked out at the statues that surrounded a stream. A fountain spouted water into the rain. Antonio opened the door to the servant's quarters. It was huge. He turned on the light and walked up two flights of stone stairs to a small glass door.

Opening it for me, he motioned me to the right, down a long corridor, which was covered in artwork. He opened a door and said that this room was mine, and put my bag on the bed. He told me that we should start eating dinner because he was hungry and made his way to the kitchen. I sat on the duvet-covered bed and looked at the photographs of his daughter, which decorated the room. Some of her teenage artwork hung on the walls. A bulky wood armoire took up a good part of the narrow room. I found the bathroom next door and washed my hands in the cold water. Antonio did not have much heat on in the servant's part of the villa. Probably too expensive to heat for one lonely guy. He called my name and after taking a pee, I walked into the dining room to greet him.

Knowing I was vegetarian from our last lunch, he placed some crackers on the table with asiago and parmesan cheeses. More cheese. How fattening. Ever since I had met Barb, I had tried to keep my weight under 150 pounds. She was lovely and conscious of her weight. I was a big girl, about 160, then. Before I met her, I ate anything I wanted—pork ribs, French fries, Reeses Peanut Butter Cups. As I am approaching middle age, I have begun jogging and stopped eating meat. Every time I sit down to eat, I stress out about what it is, and how much it will cost me. My cholesterol is down, certainly. Keeping myself at 150 is not an easy task. Antonio said that cheese was not fattening, especially if you eat it with some fine wine from the region. He said that the wine cuts through the fat—and with a chuckle, that the fat cuts through the wine. He said that I never refuse a drink. Who can in Italy? I may be a directionless blob, but I am not unappreciative of fine things. Wine in Italy is like basketball in the U.S.

He set the table for four and brought out the good china and silverware. He placed the presents on the table and lit two long candles. As we sat down, when we heard a car pull up and come sloshing to a stop.

"They are here." He got up and went down to the front door. I took a look at the artwork on the walls. My view of art and music is completely sensual: it is good if it makes my senses tingle. Was this a result of years of study or reading about art, seeing things, leafing through my dad's picture books? Playing the piano? I loved all the pieces Antonio had on his wall. None were pretentious—all felt painted by people who do not do it for a living, but rather for the love of it. Not to be famous, but to be famed, adored, famished, hungry. For love, not an agent. *Amare, amateur.* Love, amateur. They have the same root.

Many a moment I have wrestled with myself about what it means to be an artist. Barb says that artists are pretentious people, because everyone is an artist. They aren't special. I wanted her to say, "You aren't special." Or better yet, "You are an artist and you are special." We did not have any artist friends. I think that artists are people who are consumed by their own mortality. That's why we have to create all the time: fear that we are going to die without leaving anything behind. The artist is kind of a new word. Bach wasn't an artist; he was a music maker. Raphael was a painter. These days Sting is an artist, Madonna and Run DMC are artists. Even Bill Clinton is an artist. It's become a label for leftwing, "out there" politics. It has been consumed by rightwing America to designate people who don't conform. It was been watered down to mean anything you want it to. The Artist Formerly Known as Prince.

I heard footsteps carrying heavy bags up the steps. A cheerful, plump couple walked in with pleasant auras, each shook my hand. Antonio led them to their rooms and I sat back down to my bottle of prosecco. Antonio came back into the room with a pot of vegetable soup, which he made especially for me. It looked like the vegetables came right from the premises. Greens, leeks, parsley, potatoes—he spooned some in each of our bowls and handed us some crackers. His family was clearly spent by Italian traffic.

"We've been driving for five hours from Milan. That's too long," Maria said. She looked so kind, I hoped that she had had thoughts of kissing women at some point in her life. Probably not. Or in Italy, girls have them before they hit fifteen, after kissing their best friends, then they straighten themselves out. Find a *ragazzo* (boyfriend). I had. Maria said that they had had something to eat with her mother and weren't particularly hungry—it was midnight after all. I was famished and spooned down three helpings of soup with splashes of wine.

Antonio's son was particularly sensitive. He said very little and winked a lot at me, while his father told story after story about Alitalia and how he brought his children chocolate from South Africa. We had connected. I began to ask Maria questions about her family while Antonio told his stories because I was going a little crazy. When she responded that she had grown up in Milan and that she knew that tomorrow was Yom Kippur, Antonio looked surprised and said that he did not know that she was Jewish. She never told him. She said that her father was of Romanian descent and that they celebrated the high holidays.

"Really. Why didn't you tell me?" he asked.

She said nothing and received a wink from the son, Sergio.

Antonio continued to chat about the Dolomites and Pecorino cheese, when I noticed the candle flicker.

"There is a ghost in here," I said boldly.

Everyone looked at me intently.

"I can see ghosts, you know."

Antonio smiled a great big smile.

"I have been seeing them in Pennsylvania, when I ride my bicycle to school through the cemetery."

Antonio continued to smile and in the same moment began to talk about Yom Kippur. "What do people do on Yom Kippur?" he asked me.

"Go to synagogue, pray and fast. It's so that you take the day and contemplate your actions during the last year."

"Seems a little extreme," he volunteered.

"It works. By the end of the hungry day, you remember how good you have it. I can eat when I want. Take a bath. Chat with a friend. In the last years I've begun to think that God exists—how I am not sure. Ritual at home and in synagogue helps to remember. Helps to recall a world beyond the one that we can see."

The table members seemed to get more and more uncomfortable with my talk. The wine was affecting my sense of propriety, and I was waxing more honest than usual. I ate some cookies and finished my glass of wine—it was finally time to go to bed. Antonio gave me some towels and a wish for a *buona notte* (good night). I asked if I could help wash the dishes. He said no, no, that was his job and he did it happily. Sergio winked and said that Antonio is very particular about how things get done in his house. I brushed my teeth and took a look at my blemishes in the clean mirror. Vowing not to bend at temptation, I did not pick my face, and thought I would feel better about that in the morning. The anxiety of being at the college had dissipated and I did not feel the urgency of picking my face to make myself calm down. I felt calm, but annoyed with Antonio, and slightly scared of him. He was sticky, like lemon juice. My room was cold and I went to sleep in my pants and a sweater.

Chapter 5

It continued to rain the next day. The light filtered through my window and behind it a cloud of gray as made me feel as if were on an airplane. I got up and looked out the window to see a dilapidated courtyard, surrounded on three sides by hallways. An old horse-carriage stood in the corner. Red clay tiles covered the roof. My watch said eight-thirty, and I feared that I had slept through breakfast. Antonio wakes up at five every morning to feed the geese and chase away the great blue herons that come swooping down to eat the goldfish he had plopped in the pond.

I dug out my *nino* and decided to give Valeria a quick call, to see how she was feeling. She picked up in a high-pitched voice, saying that she was happy to hear from me and eager to visit me in Venice. I told her about Antonio and the villa with some trepidation. Sometimes in strange places I have a deep-seated feeling that I will never return to normalcy. A sickening feeling envelops me and, as I have described to my shrink several times, it feels as if someone is standing on my heart. Often it is accompanied by a painful sensation in my wrists, as if they are burning. I have spent much of my life trying to avoid these sensations, which were much more marked around my mother than in any other situations. Then came my shortness of breath, followed by a deep sense of urgency that it should stop immediately.

Valeria told me that she had spoken to her sister's shrink,

who said that she had tried everything to veer her off the path of self-destruction. She had prescribed anti-anxiety medication and anti-depression medication. She had met her twice a week to comfort her. But there was no going back. An odd calm overtook Angela once she decided to commit the act. She would smile incoherently at sad news, laugh in the middle of a sentence, and began to wear excessive make-up and fashionable clothes. Her vision of the afterlife was like a mud bath in a ritzy Italian spa. No flames, no regrets. The shrink said that she had tried to kill herself on two previous occasions. First she stood on a bridge in the middle of the night, futilely urging her will to jump. Fear of bodily harm overtook her, and she walked slowly back to her car and drove home. The second time she thought that she would walk in front of an oncoming train. She hesitated at the last minute and began opting again for a less violent death. Before the suicide, Angela had stopped eating and spoke very little. "I am so sad that I did not see her before she died," Valerie admitted.

"When was the last time you saw her?"

"About six weeks before she died. I ran into her in the piazza. I smiled at her and stopped, and she just walked right by me."

"How awful."

"That is my last memory of her. I had know idea how sick she was." She held back a sob.

"I am so sorry."

"I will feel better. Do not worry. Cesare is taking care of me now."

"I am glad. Listen, call me anytime. Anyway, will we see each other in a couple of weeks?"

"Yes, I will come to Venice."

"Good. Take care, my friend," I said and hung up. I was typically abrupt, and got this habit from my parents, who were always concerned about the long distance bill.

I grabbed some fresh clothes, my toothbrush, and a towel and went into the bathroom. I hadn't taken a shower in a week (I had taken sponge baths!) and wanted to take full advantage of this luxury. When you are feeling blue, remember how lucky you are to be able to take showers. Take one and feel the luxury. Who needs a luxury car when you have a shower? Antonio's bathroom had none of the pizzazz of many Italian bathrooms. It was vintage 1974, bland and functional. And was it cold in there. I turned on the hot water as far as it would go and waited for the room to steam up a bit. No way could I wash my thick hair in that drippy water. So I didn't, but worried that my hair would smell bad to my host. I don't think Italians really mind bodily odors. They mind ugly clothes. The soap felt as if it had been last used in 1974, and I sensed that his daughter's presence was all around me. She used to clean herself here, in a fit of despair. Cleaning and crying go together like bows and arrows. I began cleaning in between each of my toes only after I met Barb. She said my feet stank and I had to do something. It had never occurred to me to clean between the toes, since that required bending and my back was sore after so many years of soccer.

Showered and red-skinned, I put my clothes on and walked into the dining room, where Sergio was reading the newspaper. I could smell coffee on the stove.

"*Buon giorno*," he saluted me. "Did you sleep well?"

"Yes," sweetheart, I wanted to say.

"It is cold in here. I have a mind to turn on the heat."

"I wish you would," I said looking for my jacket and a hat. "Any news about the Formula 1 race? Do you think that Ferrari can really pull it off?"

He seemed stunned that I cared about sports, and said,

"Yes."

Sergio was clearly a person of few words. Like a skinny person in a donut factory, he was rebelling against his environment.

Maria came in all rumpled and tired. She did not take a shower—as it was not customary before breakfast in Italy, or after. Coffee was on her mind and she asked Antonio for some in the kitchen. I heard them laugh, and I walked in to see if I could make myself some tea to warm up my rainy bones. Bowls of shelled walnuts in jars lined the counters. I began to eat some.

"They are from the villa's property," Antonio said. "I have been gathering them for weeks. Look at my hands." He laid out his fingers in front of us and they looked like those of a painter, covered in dark ink. "The walnuts do this to them. It's very hard to get off."

Maria continued to chat about their flat in London near Hyde Park. They must make big bucks if they live there, I thought. Jealous, I suppose, since my house was modest, because my college kept my salary low—they could. I was a music a professor and we are a dime a dozen. Music professors are the least paid of all faculty members in universities, an ex-lover smugly told me recently. Things were not going to improve soon, especially after the dean of faculty told me in all her wisdom that sciences are what count in a small college. "They help create an endowment. Look at Sarah Lawrence," she said earnestly. "They put all their eggs into the art scene basket and they have no endowment." How discouraging. Academia. Oy vei. No, stop! I am on sabbatical in Italy. Nothing's going to bring me down.

After breakfast Antonio asked me if I wanted a tour of his grounds and villa. His kids were going into town to renew some documents, and we would have the morning to ourselves.

Not knowing what else to do and interested anyway, I agreed on one condition—that he find me a pair of boots to walk in the mud. Antonio went around in his clogs, and there was no way that I was going to ruin my shoes doing the same. He found a pair of green boots that reached my knees and I bundled up under a trusty raincoat, and out the door we went.

First he took me behind the villa to show me his fruit and walnut trees. There must have been forty or so trees in all, and he took enormous pride in showing me how many new walnut trees had sprouted only in the last years, like weeds. They were producing walnuts galore. He bent down to retrieve more and gave me a couple too. He cracked them between his hands and shoved the contents in his mouth. "These are spectacular," he said. I followed him through the saturated grounds, while he said wistfully that maintaining order in the orchard was beyond his means and time. "Foxes and little bunnies live among the trees. Birds from all over Europe stop here for a few days before continuing their journey to the Mediterranean." We then moved to the manicured garden in the front of the villa, where I had noticed the statues the night before. We walked over the small stream that traversed the property.

"Why did people put statues in their gardens?" I asked. "And who are they, anyway?" I braced myself for a dissertation-long response.

"They are a sign of nobility and education. Each is of a Roman or Renaissance poet." We walked over and read "Virgilio" at the base of one.

"No women here, I suppose," I pondered.

He did not respond. Poetry was not a woman's task, at least for Italians.

We walked by Horace and Marsilio Ficino. Each held a book and looked into the distance. They were admiring his villa, I am sure. They were commenting on his sense of justice and his noble intellect. Antonio stopped in front of Mussato. "Now here was a great man. A Paduan statesman, playwright, soldier. Look how the sculptor captured his character." I thought that Antonio was going to have an orgasm.

We watched the geese meander down into the stream and come back out. They were wary of us, even though Antonio fed them every day. He said that they weren't particularly friendly, but they weren't stupid either. "*La sciagurata* gave me these two," he pointed to two big geese. "She got them from a farm of a friend of hers. I loved her then. She was a vegetarian and loved animals. Just like you," Antonio said. "She came to the villa on the weekends. She cooked for me. We drank wine. We were engaged."

"How long did you know her?"

"Two months."

"Isn't that a little quick to get engaged?"

"I was right for her. She could have moved her business into the horse's quarters. I'll show it to you. It's huge. I could have insulated it. She could have been happy here. I would have done anything for her."

Except listen to her, I thought. I could not stand it anymore and said, "You need to learn how to listen."

"I listen just fine. Much better than most of my friends. I am interested in what she has to say. I worship the ground she walks on. She should have stayed here with me."

It was pointless, like trying to convince a child that Teletubbies were boring.

He walked me around the river to the far end of his property. The sound of city traffic infiltrated the pastoral paradise. A cement wall separated his dream from another's reality. He bent down to pick up some trash that had been dumped on his side. I collected some candy wrappers and broken glass bottles. Antonio told me to throw them over the fence on the street. I couldn't, so he grabbed the bottles out of my hand, chucked them over, and smiled when they smashed to pieces on the other side of the street. No wonder people threw stuff on this property. He told me that he had an old rifle and that he would us it to scare the next kid who did that. He would stand in the trees and come running out at the kid with the rifle. Sounded like a goofy idea, but he would never listen to me.

Antonio said that he wanted to show me the stables and the villa proper. He walked his soggy clogs into the house and asked me to take my boots off. I began to feel that I was passing time with my dead grandfather. As a child I used to listen to him describe the musty houses he owned. I enjoyed our lazy afternoons together inspecting his property in the Alps. I asked smart questions, and he was delighted with my childish curiosity. Antonio led me to the villa's stables. He showed me where the horses were fitted with hoofs and how the straw was placed into bins for them to eat. He took me to an enormously large rectangular room, where the servants made wool for the villa's occupants. *La sciagurata* was to have worked here. How? It was so lonely and damp. Antonio showed me the wooden planks that served to dry the wool in the summer. We walked up rickety stairs to a spacious, windowed room that served as the servants' quarters. Antonio wanted to turn this into a guesthouse. He always had visitors to the villa over the summer, usually from Germany and Britain. They could sleep here, all together. It was warmer and sunnier here, with plenty of space. Old gals often came to inquire about Antonio's villa, and I can imagine that they fell in love with the former Alitalia pilot, until he wouldn't stop talking, and then they ran back to their homelands, shaking their heads. British women loved the gardens and fantasized about a prince in knight's clothing. Instead they got a pilot who couldn't shut up.

These rooms were large and wooden, like refuges in the Italian Alps, or barracks. Antonio dreamed of life with his maid Marion, away from the hassles and toils of the Italian bourgeoisie, but near enough to grab some dinner and see an art exhibit once in a while. The place smelled of cement and walnuts, ceramic bricks and stables. It smelled of unfinished business and dreams. Antonio was a divorced knight, a lonely prince. I felt myself transported back to my childhood listening to my grandfather complain about Italian politics, and loving the Queen of England to the point that he made his family stand up when she was on television. We then walked through the courtyard and in the front door.

"Let me show you the primary part of the villa," Antonio said, taking out a ten-inch key from his pocket. He shoved the enormous iron key inside the wooden door, wiggled it around and pushed the door open. We walked in and felt the dampness. The maroon-colored walls were covered with paintings. The ceilings had vestiges of frescoes. He said the paintings were *trump d'oeils*—mirages, or heavenly landscapes. All looked as if they had been painted by Watteau.

"Whose paintings are these?" I naturally inquired.

"They are from an exhibit I had here a couple of months ago. The artists haven't come to pick them up."

Large canvases with thick paint hung on the walls. Most were of dark landscapes and mountain vistas. He pointed to one in particular, by his friend Mauro Brindelli, a genius, he said. I always get nervous when I hear people call others geniuses. Women and people of color are rarely called that in our culture, though we are competent, hard working and visionary. I suppose you could translate visionary into genius.

"I love the way he paints the chariot in the sky," Antonio said.

"Have you ever thought of painting?" I asked.

"I have no talent for drawing."

"How do you know if you never tried?" I said, sounding very American.

"I have no feel for it."

"It's about the process. Maybe you would love doing it."

"No."

"I paint, and I have no natural talent."

"It's not right."

"Why? When I sit down and take time to mix my paints, plan a picture, it feels right." What I was saying now was truly Disney. For Italians, painting was a craft, a life's work, a thing you learned as a child and did for a living. Not something you did at a community college after work.

"Do you like this one?"

"I think that you should get some paints and paint. You feel it so deeply. You are an artist at heart." I felt sorry for Antonio and liked his honesty.

He returned the subject to his friend, blah blah, and I wondered about what I just said. How did I know that he was an artist? What was I feeling from him? An energy, an excitement and devotion to understanding the human condition? An aura? He did have a blue light around him. I saw it come to life in the villa.

"Antonio, have you ever had your cards read?"

"No."

"It's really not that big a deal. I had my students doing them in my medieval music and culture class at the college. They were each required to purchase a deck. Then they had to read their histories and assign a piece of music to each face card.

The chairman of the department popped his head in, smiling. "It's medieval games day," I said, trying to cover my tracks. "I am teaching them some medieval ways to pass time."

Drawn to the spiritual even in my academic work, I once wrote an article about the role of music in astrology. In medieval Italy, those born under the signs of Virgo, Libra, and Taurus were deemed "most musical." Sagittarius and Capricorn least so. If you are born during the sign of Libra, making music will be for relaxing and cultivating beautiful and more intellectual things—a kind of pastime for cultured aristocrats. If you are born under the sign of Taurus, your music making will be sensuous and naughty and fun. You will play music to seduce people. It will most probably lead to sex.

Then I told Antonio to go to a shrink. It just came out of my mouth, like a curse after getting cut off on the highway. "It would help. You seem to be in so much pain."

"I don't believe in them. My ex-brother-in-law was one. And he is crazy, like his sister."

"You just need to find the right one."

"I think that they are useless. I know what is the matter with me."

"I am living proof that they help. No matter what you say. I was a walking wreck, and now, after ten years of therapy, I can face each day and even dream about the next one."

"They are paid to do nothing but listen."

I was talking to myself again. "They can help you take responsibility for your own actions and improve your life."

"My life is fine. Much better since I split up from my wife. Believe me. She was the cause of most of my problems. Spoiled girl. Now she has turned my own daughter against me."

Useless. "Antonio, I'm going to buy you a book. Is there a bookstore in town? In Belluno?

"Yes, let's go there. I think that Paolo wanted to do some shopping in Belluno later. Buy himself a nice suit."

"It's written by the Dalai Lama and a shrink. *The Art of Happiness* teaches you how to be a more compassionate and loving person. It shows you how to be a better person, thus becoming a happier person." I could have been talking to my dog, Honey, or my mother.

We walked up a flight of stairs into a dining room. A big oak table filled the room, with ten chairs on either side of it. A fireplace big enough to stand up in flanked it on one side. "The British had a big party here," he said. "They got smashed."

We walked into the kitchen. It had two fireplaces and was lined with silver and brass pots and pans. There were two sinks and a large oven. A kitchen for kings, I thought. In my imagination, servants came running in and out carrying trays of food and carafes of wine. Impatient ladies of the mansion instructed them to move faster. Now the villa was empty, except for an occasional ghost. I told Antonio this, and he smiled. But I wasn't laughing. Out the corner of my eye, I saw a small female ghost crouching over the sink, washing. She had on a powder blue sweater. Her long dark hair was pulled back into a ponytail. She was washing the dishes, happily and quietly. Antonio showed me the cast iron stove and the ancient bread pans and the forms for making cheese. Cobwebs connected everything together like tissue. The ghost lifted her head and told me everything was going to be OK. Just calm down, she said. You have nothing to fear. I thanked her in my mind and continued to hear Antonio's voice explain the way the stove worked and how he intends to transform the entire floor into a bed and breakfast for British gals. "I can cook up some eggs and toast in the mornings. I cook pretty well indeed." I couldn't argue here—his cooking was simple, yet tasty, with little fat, yet rich. "Tonight, I make you ravioli with fennel and artichoke sauce. It is splendid. You will no doubt say that to me." Now he was composing my sentences too. Just like Clara Schumann's father, Frederick, had done for her in her diary. He wrote her diary, and she didn't begin to speak until she was eight. He taught her theory and harmony at age four and fancied her another Mozart. Unlike Mozart, she stopped speaking.

Antonio showed me the inside of the stove with its massive iron grating. "You can cook six chickens in here," as if I really wanted to hear that, a vegetarian with a phobia about ovens. Ovens meant death to me, not life, not parties. He shut the door to the kitchen, and we walked up another flight of stairs. Here was an enormous sitting room, with fourteen-foot ceilings covered with artwork. A beat-up harpsichord was in the corner. I went over to it immediately—struck a few keys and heard only thumping noises. "It doesn't work," he said. As if I couldn't tell. It would have been nice to play, improvise a little at that very instant. I was so anxious that only music, wine, teaching, or writing could calm me down. Center me again. Stop me from being terrified of being in the villa. Stop the panic attack that was enveloping my heart like a jealous dog. Sadness so deep it was biting. Out of the corner of my eye, I saw the female ghost enter the room. This time she sat down on a chair and gave me a good look. She smiled reassuringly, spoke quietly. "Speak to him."

I interrupted Antonio's rambles with a story about the time my grandfather took me to see his cabin in the mountains. He made me a bowl of plain rice and a cheese sandwich. He took me on a short hike on the path labeled #9. It went as far as the top of the Gran Paradiso. We would climb that together one day, he insisted. I told him about the color of the mountain flowers that sprouted an inch off the ground, everything in miniature like a charm bracelet. Antonio started up about flowers, but this time I wouldn't let him. "Please, Antonio, I need you to listen to me." And I told him about the time I slid down the slope for miles on my butt. The time my mother forbade me from going on the glacier. I just kept on going, seeing in my head things that had happened in the Italian Alps, as Antonio and I walked aimlessly around the villa. I told him a longer story, just to see if he could listen. It is called "Uncle Riccardo's Driving Lesson" and it was published in *Fiammetta*, the second installment of my trilogy. It's basically about *Fiammetta* driving an old Alfa across the Alps from Switzerland to Italy.

Antonio listened to the very end, without lifting his head or asking a question, as if he had gone into a trance.

I woke him up with the phrase, "Dad can be a nasty guy."

Antonio replied that Dad isn't mean, he just loses his patience. Stop, Antonio, now you listen to me. "I never said that he was a bad guy. He just gets angry with me for no reason, because I forgot to take out the trash, or flush the toilet. He screams at me still—but especially when I was a child." Soon after talking and stopping Antonio from talking, the thick veil of sadness began to melt away. The monster stepped off my chest. Talking, expressing myself, telling a story proved to be the antidote and I had to thank the ghost, whose name I believe was Hilda. She was of Austrian descent, from Salzburg and stayed on in Feltre after the Austrian's defeat in WWI. She was indebted to the lady of the house at that time, Zelda.

Writing is like describing ghosts.

But not like describing dreams. Dreams are otherworldly, ghosts are real. Now how does that make sense? But it does if you sit and listen to your heart. Dreams can't tell the future, they can tell the present. They tell you how you feel when you don't even know it. Ghosts can tell you about the past and the future. Your disasters and your dreams.

Antonio led me back down the steps outside and around the front of the villa. Below the main stairs was a door, which he unlatched. "You must hear this to believe it. But first, look," he said pointing to the corner. "I want to install a fountain in here, the one that originally sat in the middle of the other room. Imagine, a fountain inside the home—absolute luxury." And insanity, I thought. It will make things so humid. A rich friend of mine installed a lap pool in her brownstone. The walls dripped. Antonio brought me into a rectangular basement and stood in the middle saying, "Listen," and sang a line from Mozart's opera *Don Giovanni*. "Can you believe these acoustics? Clear. My, this is fabulous," and he sang another line. I saw something stir in the corner. It was a mouse. "I am going to have a concert series down here. My musician friend, Gino, said it was perfect. I could fit at least a hundred chairs." Antonio was a dreamer with a long line of friends who spent one night at his villa and never again spoke to him. He told me himself. "I entertained him here a whole weekend. Drove him to the mountains. Made him dinner. You would think that he would call me when he comes to Venice. I heard that he was just here a month ago to do a series of concerts. Not a word."

While Antonio was talking, I thought about my relationship to my father. I had no feminine regret about not listening to Antonio. I had essentially followed in Dad's footsteps. We are both academics. But he is well known. I am not. He has a big job in a prestigious university. I do not. I swim in anonymity, thinking that I should have accomplished more than I have. The academic community does not embrace me because few people understand me. I am not asked to give papers on panels or contribute articles to books. When I go to an academic conference, I feel numb, like bouncing around Macy's during the Christmas season. When the college's low-level administrators remind me that I am not cherished by the people in my field, I get frightened and think that I am stupid and undeserving. They are right. Everyone else is right about me and my life. Jean, you need to leave that little Pennsylvania school. They don't pay you much, they don't respect you in your department. They marginalize you, my mother tells me—and I remind myself each time that I am not included in a discussion about salary or a new faculty hire.

My strength is in teaching—there I cannot be attacked. Did I mention that I won a teaching award at the college? Best Teacher—as voted by the students. My favorite thing in the world is the gift of getting in front of a class, or helping a student with a problem. My acne clears up in a matter of minutes when I am teaching. The worry that my career is not progressing as fast as it should dissipates, and I am so in the moment that my mother could be yelling at me to use the kind of toothpaste that whitens your teeth because they are yellow during my class and I wouldn't even hear. My assignments are considered "unserious" by the dean, who can no longer sabotage me because I have tenure. For a history of the United States class, I asked students to design a garden and put their favorite things in it. I was summoned to the dean's office after I had the class produce an original opera based on something, anything they had learned in the class. So they wrote about Hillary Clinton sleeping with Plato, who was in love with Jefferson. Hillary killed Plato when she found out, and did a striptease after the crime. Brilliant, I thought.

"You are not serious," stammered the dean. I listened to him, and felt taken over by a voice telling me that when I contemplated having the students write a gossip column

about Plato rather than the required essay comparing Plato and
Aristotle, it was right. It felt right. Then caution goes to the
wind, as I read poetry and show them how to dance and tell
them to listen to their inner voice—that it has the answers.
When I listen, it says, "Just be yourself."

This can be lonely.

So I try to make it by being an incredibly sensitive and "nice"
person. Which really weirds people out. "Who the hell is that
half-baked individual? She is not who she thinks she is!" But
my real personality leaks out. I am vibrant and full of life.
Full of my own visions and almost forty, though I haven't
even scratched the surface of them. I am living my father's
life. Living out my mother's wishes of being a confident and
successful academic. The fact is I am a woman, which in
an academic environment means sleeping with male faculty,
writing about the "Masters of Music." Being the good girl
professor.

When you think about it, my mother's generation cannot
really conceive of what it takes to make it as an unmarried
person. Success means finding a husband, a powerful man who,
incidentally, she calls a pig, and who gives you money and
many children, and takes care of familial business. He probably
has a girlfriend on the side, as my dad does. Italians don't
marry for love, at least the ones I know. My mother achieved
power through my father's connections: she met the prime
minister of Italy when Dad was knighted, and the president of
Columbia University when he received an award for excellence
in scholarship. Yet she is his boss and has the ability to beat
him into submission with a biting comment, like "you are just
as stupid as before you got your Ph.D.," and "I never liked that
ugly poem anyway," after his award-winning article about the
relationship between Michelangelo's Pietà and Shakespeare's

sonnets was published. Her success means that for whatever reason, he does not leave her alone when she is fifty. Mom is much more successful than her friends, who are either dead or divorced. For her it is the same thing. My mother is my father's mother, too: she cleans his clothes and tells him to sit straight at the table and rips off the dry-cleaning tag on his pants in a fancy restaurant. Dad complies and then sleeps with his assistant, who wears tight clothing to work every day and stands too close to him. I don't do any of this stuff, and if I am so high and noble and have friends, a wonderful partner, a good job, and a nice dog, why am I so miserable?

Antonio locked the door of the villa behind me and escorted me back into the servants' quarters. His son was back home and they were waiting to take a drive into Belluno to buy some clothes. They had a black, sleek station wagon Audi, and the women sat in the back while the men sat in silence. We looked at the bases of the mountains through the raindrops. Antonio extolled my father's persona and I felt ill. Giotto's daughter I was and will ever be.

We walked around Belluno and into a dark cathedral. Art was much darker here than in Tuscany. Madonna's looked gaunt, as if they had grown up on the streets of New York City. They had long, skinny faces and their babies looked pensive and lugubrious. Saints of little renown drawn by *klein meisters*. Antonio said that one was by Bellini in the fifteenth century, but when we walked up to the little sign that explained the picture and gave a brief history, we found out that it was by Giacomo in the seventeenth century. "Look, that statue is by Gandolfi in the eighteenth century," Antonio said. It was by Piero in the fifteenth century. I stopped listening.

I dragged him to the local bookstore, while his family went looking for Italian suits. "Do you have the newest book by the

Dalai Lama?" I asked the female bookstore owner. Antonio said that they would never have it here—why would they? The little lady insisted that they had everything; it was just a matter of looking. Italian bookstores aren't arranged like Barnes and Noble. They don't have tidy signs saying Fiction, Biography, Sports. It's all mixed up in a minestrone, and only the owner knows the ingredients. I flipped through a number of titles. It was very hard for me to read these days. It seemed like I was wasting time. I thought that I was going to die soon, and had to write my scholarly stuff so that I would be famous in a very limited circle, like being the best-dressed handler at the local dog show.

"The best thing to do to get a novel published is to talk about sex. Or betrayal or murder. A book without any of these will not make it to the Oprah Book Club list, or break into the Best Seller list. If one wants to make art that speaks from the soul, with the honesty of a family photograph, be assured that you need to keep your day job." A tidbit from an impatient writer friend.

My mind wandered in Antonio's presence—his talking had become meditative, like the tape of waves at the Oregon Coast my shrink had given me when I couldn't sleep during my tenure battle. The owner of the bookstore was listening to Antonio tell her what her home town was like in Tuscany. He spoke of the fish in the sea, and the woman said a word and he said a litany of things about who real Tuscans are. After a while my book appeared and the owner shook Antonio's hand and said, "You don't know what a great favor you have done for me. Talking about my home. I miss it so." I paid for the book, which was routinely wrapped in a piece of paper, and Antonio said, "Isn't it wonderful how people tell me their stories?" Maybe I should start talking more. It may be that some of the reason for my virtual silence as a child comes from the fact that I had to speak in Italian on many occasions. I didn't have a complete command of the vocabulary, and probably sounded a bit American, so I didn't speak around my mother's friends. Bi-culturalism can be as infuriating as bi-sexuality. Only, there are more clubs for bi-sexuals these days.

I told Antonio to read the book and try to take more responsibility for his choices and his life. We stood by a promontory and looked out into the mist. He held an umbrella above my head. "I am miserable without *La sciagurata*. She has permanently wounded me. That awful woman. How could she have done this to me?" I struggled to find an appropriate passage to fix Antonio's problem in the Dalai Lama book, but to no avail. If I recall, in the Dalai Lama's philosophy one should be compassionate for the suffering of others and struggle to improve one's life through forgiveness and hard work. Forgive the bastards at the college for my tenure hell. Forgive my parents. Forgive a guy for cutting me off on the street. Or my brother for calling me a dyke. Wait a second. Forgiving did not elevate me out of depression, it felt heavy and difficult. What did make me feel better was a glass of wine. Antonio was not about to forgive anybody for his misery, and somehow I couldn't fault him. If forgiveness was so great, why did I feel so awful? I had forgiven everybody. Ask my shrink. We met his family back at the car and drove in silence back to the soggy villa.

The next morning his son and daughter-in-law left at seven in the morning, which was excessive to me. I thought a weekend with my parents was long—they left after just twenty-four hours, and were mostly silent. No "How are you?"s were exchanged during these twenty-four hours. So un-American. Antonio said that I was extremely lucky to have been born into two cultures, to which I replied that I am never happy where I am. "You have a unique polyphony of viewpoints that can't be taught later on. It's like learning an instrument at a young age." This sounded amazing, and I was very touched and flattered and thought about how lucky I was that when I am in the United States I miss Italy and *vice versa.*

Antonio asked me if I wanted to go with his friends Anna and Mario, whom we had met Friday night, to see an art exhibit in a villa in the Friuli. He asked me whether it was OK to take another day away from my studies, and I said sure, having immersed myself in the study of something completely different, and which had little to do with computers and dusty libraries. "How will I get back to Venice?" I asked.

"I'll drop you off," he said, picking up the phone and finalizing plans with Anna.

I gathered my pajamas and bathroom stuff and brought them into the sitting room. Antonio found the invitation to the exhibit and we walked down the stairs. "I don't like her boyfriend. One bit."

We drove through the rainy countryside along the deep valley of the Adige River. An old train chugged beside us. I said that it was a *littorina*, proud of remembering those small steam trains I had seen in the Valle d'Aosta. Antonio said they are called that because they were made in the city of *Littoria* in Fascist time.

We wound our way up to Anna's villa and drove into the driveway after she opened the automatic gate. She and her boyfriend were ready and happy that Antonio had brought them a basket of walnuts. She smiled at me sympathetically, as if I had just completed volunteer work picking up garbage on the side of a highway. I got a better look at her in the daytime. She was typically Italian: her hair was colored in gray and brown streaks, her nails were clear, her pants and shirt colorful and tight. She was overly tan, I would say bronzed. Her nose was huge and she had big blue eyes. On her wrists hung thick gold jewelry. Gold rings with fat stones decorated her skinny fingers, made skinnier by constant exercise. She was an exercise bulimic, I thought. Never stood still and ate a lot. Her knees creaked when she got into the back seat of the car with Bob, her dachshund. Italians inevitably give their dogs English names. Anna had Antonio's nuts in her hand. She put two walnuts together and tried to crack them open. I tried too. Then we passed them to Antonio in the front seat, who cracked them immediately, which made him feel more like a man.

Anna never looked at me when she spoke. She did not speak to me and she did not respond when I asked her a question. At one point she did ask, "Why is your Italian so good?" When I responded, she started talking about a villa we had just passed and the bank that was funding its restoration. That's what folks in the Veneto did on the weekends, villa hop. Mine is better than yours. Mine has a bigger garden. Villas bumped right up against the main highways, looking very French or Austrian. They were rectangular in the front, with two long passageways extending behind them. That was typical, Antonio said. "Shouldn't you know that?" Well, sorry.

We drove by the town of Pordenone, and Anna said that her grandma owned a castle just to the north of it, where she and her sister used to play hide-and-seek in its enormous rooms on Saturdays. She said that the family recently sold it, because the upkeep was way too high. "Villas are very expensive to maintain. The heat alone could send a rich person into the poorhouse," she said scratching her big right nostril. "My father, bless his soul, sold it before he died." She told me that he had died of prostate cancer. He was a strong man, big shouldered, and carried on the tradition of glass making. Her dog began to lick my hand and I gave it a piece of walnut.

"Don't you want to eat that?" she said.

"He might like some."

"It's a waste. Give it to me, I'll eat it." I crushed more walnuts for her in my hand, removed the shells and gave them to her. I would do anything now to gain her favor. She didn't give me the time of day. How attractive. Antonio stopped an old man on his bicycle to ask for directions to the villa. The old man, who must have served in the army because he seemed so sure of himself and happy with his life's sacrifices (either that or he had a mistress), gave a long set of directions that no one bothered to listen to, so we stopped a guy driving his BMW. "Straight and then make a left and a right." He made me smile. My mother could never get right and left straight. It was inevitably the opposite of what she said, and the last time she yelled at me for laughing when I said "Right?" and she said "Left" but she really meant right. She said, "I have a problem. You shouldn't laugh at me."

We followed a narrow road until we reached a dark-skinned man walking. Anna said, "He won't know anything," but Antonio stopped anyway and gave the guy a chance. "It's right behind you, over there." Antonio thanked him wholeheartedly and Anna shook her head, hoping the man would go back to wherever he came from. Her bitchiness was contagious, like a yawn. I started getting crabby. We parked the car, shook out our legs and walked through a gate. I felt particularly underdressed and un-Italian, my hair streaked with gray, my jeans baggy, my shoes sneakers. Anna knew the owners and was great with kisses. She let the dachshund down to piss in the courtyard.

Antonio, with his jacket hanging over his shoulder, unleashed a litany of compliments to the hostess. I asked for the bathroom. People hold their pee for a lot longer in Italy than in the United States. Americans are concerned that we will get some kind of cancer or infection. My students bring gallons of water to class, and need to leave class to pee all the time. The villa's john was clean and cold as I sat on it. I usually squat over the bowl, but I let caution to the wind in this instance and put one cheek on the seat cover. I washed my hands and ran back to my new friends.

"This is Jean D'Entreves, an American. She is a professor at a college," Antonio said, introducing me valiantly to an older woman.

"Nice to meet you," I said and smiled. They moved on to other guests and I moved to the table full of prosecco glasses. Two went down my throat within two minutes, one for being too tall and one for feeling American. Then I noticed a total queen walk in with a fluffy white dog. His hands were waving in the air as if he were about to faint. He wasn't, he just wanted to eat more homemade sausage, cut in thick slices near the prosecco. He was probably married—who knows. I walked over to the table and picked up a hunk of Parmesan cheese on a toothpick and stuffed it into my mouth.

Two women were exhibiting their artwork in the corner. The first was young, and her résumé said "Milan School of Arts," in Italian. She made art for children's bedrooms. It wasn't subversive in any way, full of plump clouds and happy clowns. She smiled at the people who walked by, and I thought that she was quite talented in an untalented sort of way. She was talented for doing her own thing in Italy, even though her stuff was commercial. I congratulated her on her work and said that I was an artist, too, only that I taught in a college and didn't know what I really was. She didn't particularly care, and why should she, this was her moment to shine. Anna bought some gold jewelry from a Roman woman. Next to her was a guy selling family portraits. He had one of the Royal Family and of people important only to themselves.

They were glossy and realistic, with little dogs and bookcases. Antonio was busy chatting with the artist, who was trying to drum up some new business. I could see the allure of being immortalized in a portrait. It is so powerful, yet so passive, like using a remote control for the TV. I thought again about the kinds of compromises one has to make to be a true artist. You have to kiss your patron's ass and then have enough integrity left to speak in your own voice. A lifelong struggle that was fundamentally obvious, yet so unyielding and oppressive. Do what you want and be ready for the consequences—cope with rejection. Duh!

I walked outside and was drawn to an artificial lake. It had the requisite Italian geese and an occasional mallard. Two or more were fighting with each other and as soon as they heard me approach—geese have great hearing—they jumped into the water and began to paddle away from me. I walked over to the water and stared into its murkiness. Didn't the geese know that I haven't eaten a bird or bird by-products in years? Poplar trees and tall grasses surrounded the lake. As soon as I turned around to walk back, the geese began swimming to shore, so I played a little game of red light, green light with them. My favorite game. Antonio walked over and said that his geese might be fewer, but they were better because they had come from a breeder in Belluno and had a more elegant shape. He told me that the big ones were male and the little ones were female, and this time I was glad he was talking to me, as loneliness was seeping into my soul. I missed Barb and worried that I would never see her again. A war in the Middle East was about to burst. It would leak into Europe, with everyone taking sides and before I could hop back on a plane, they would be used as aircraft carriers and I would be stranded. It's amazing how creative worrying is. If I could just channel it into painting a picture, or doing some needlepoint.

As much as I was enjoying life in Italy, I was still longing for a life in it. If you know what I mean. You can live, but not fly, drive but not move. Anna walked over to me and asked if I liked the earrings she had just purchased for three hundred thousand lira. They are handcrafted, so is prosciutto, in Italy. Italian deli people use such care in carving and slicing their pigs. It's an art. I should have written books like Francine Mayes. Reading her books about Italy is like having Italian food in Cincinnati. You would never know the difference if you never lived there. I was waiting to be discovered. Some agent would call me up and say, "We want to publish your next thirty books." At two books a year, I could write forty in the next twenty years and place myself squarely on a literary map of fame. I could give lectures to appreciative book club members and anxious graduate students. Shouldn't self worth come from within? But it is so good to talk about getting it from the world.

Antonio had chatted with the last living person at the party. Even the dogs moved away when they saw him coming. Their ears hurt. We said that it was time to go because Prof. D'Entreves had to return to Venice to continue her studies. How thoughtful and kind. He was very considerate in certain ways. Aren't we all? Even the most evil person can be kind. That's what makes parents so puzzling. We jumped in his car and took the *autostrada* all the way to Venice. On the way to Mestre, Antonio said that he would take me to a little restaurant on the bay that catered to "my kind of people." I don't think that he was talking about bi-sexual folks. How could he tell? I had hidden it from my shrink for the first five years of therapy! Then he said that poets got together there once a week to recite what they had written. He did something my father had never done. He saw me an artist, a creative person. Bless him, I thought as he kept talking about the last time he had gone to the restaurant. He dropped me off at the Piazzale Roma in Venice. His friends ran off, and he said that he would call me. He did that night.

Chapter 6

The next few days were spent in a similar manner in Venice. I got up around eight to the sound of children running and Italian heels on the street outside my bedroom window. Like the singing of angels, these were gorgeous sounds that I had never heard before. I looked up at the ceiling, at the dark wood beams that traversed it. If I was lucky, mornings meant a welcome relief from stress. Worries did not attack me during the first fifteen minutes of each new day. My heart was light and I anticipated getting some work accomplished. After listening to morning news on my transistor radio about the escalating conflict in Israel, anxieties reappeared and I got up to take a bath.

My morning routine was long and convoluted in Venice, with no shower. Thank goodness I did not have to wash my hair today (it was still in good shape after four days), because that was an arduous process, shoving my head under the faucet and then trying to get all the hair out of the tub so as not to stuff up the drain. The tub water got murkier and murkier as I sat, and I had to refill it with hot water as it leaked slowly out. I turned up the volume on my Italian pop rock station and wondered what the people upstairs thought about my odd routine. Finished washing, even between my toes, I got out and toweled dry. I looked at my dark face in the mirror and wished that more people liked me for who I am, whoever that is. Each morning I flossed because I've had a propensity for tartar buildup. I wondered if tartar was building up in my heart valves. Then I went into the bedroom to put on my clothes, making sure that there weren't any gondoliers floating by my window who could see my bare butt, and make a habit of returning to see it every morning.

I washed all my clothes by hand in the sink because I did not want to go to the laundromat and sit and waste time. This meant drying clothes on the backs of chairs and on a makeshift clothesline I had rigged over the bathtub. The dried clothes were humid, wrinkled and rough to the touch, and had that not-quite-clean smell, no matter how long I left them steeping in the soapy water. My white gym socks absorbed the yellow wood stain from the chair on which I had dried them. A white blouse retained its dark rings round the wrists. I never attempted to wash my jeans—they would never get dry. I thought that I would wash them down in Miriam's apartment in Florence. They were gray with overuse and said American all over them.

After dressing in the same clothes I had worn the day before, I gathered my underwear and some socks, filled the sink with hot water and soap and started. I rubbed the soap into the dirty spots and ground my underwear between my hands as if grating Parmesan cheese. Especially the yellow, dried residue at the crotch. I changed the water and let them sit there with some more soap.

For breakfast I chose a piece of Pecorino cheese and a can of tuna fish. Italian tuna fish is better than American. It's moist and tasty. During the last two years, I had become overly sensitive about my weight—not wanting to carry around a caboose ass. My rear had protruded when I was a baby. My thigh muscles were big at the age of five. My mother told me I was fat, when she should have been looking in the mirror. The fact was that by now I would have become incredibly depressed if I had put that weight back on—so I attempted to prevent that and felt hungry for most of the day. Hunger reminds me of Yom Kippur fasting and has a definite connection to a higher spirit. Saints aren't overweight. When I recognized my own hunger, I thought about God.

I had a carrot too, so as to not forget my vegetables. The kitchen was dark and dirty and I quickly rinsed my utensils without looking too closely at things. I put the garbage I had made into a plastic sack. Piero, the caretaker of the building, told me that there is no recycling in Venice and to put the trash outside on the street on the side of the building. "Really?" I couldn't believe it.

"This is Venice," he smiled. "It's dirty."

I opened the door of the apartment and checked whether I had my keys. I opened the *portone*, the apartment building's primary door, and put my bag with the others on the side of the house, embarrassed at my collusion in this dirty operation. I noticed a small piece of dog poop near the garbage and smiled. We were all in this together. My *telefonino* rang when I returned, and I answered to a great big hello from Lisa. "How was the villa?" she asked. "Did he drive you crazy? Are you all right?" I answered, "Good, yes, yes" to her questions. She asked me to come to Padua that evening and spend the night. There was a nice exhibit of Bolognese painting I might like and we could go to a party afterward.

"I'd love to come. But I am going to Florence tomorrow for the weekend. Can I come see you on Tuesday, when I return? Perhaps spend the night?"

"Sure, my dear. You come whenever you wish. Stay here for weeks." This seemed excessive, as Lisa generally was.

"I will call you Monday when I better know my plans," I said, and she hung up. I did not want to commit more time because I did not want to miss one day of precious study. I had to write a paper for a history conference when I returned to the States. I hadn't started it.

Crossing the Accademia Bridge en route to the Marciana Library, I noticed it was already noon. After a stop at the Internet café to mail a few things, I saw Heimat, the Egyptian woman I had met at *La sciagurata*'s house. I called out her name as she walking along the streets. "Hello" she said cheerily, a cigarette between her fingers. "Care for some lunch?" I asked without thinking. It was my chance to talk to a real person, after a few days alone with my cellphone.

"Why not!" she said.

We immediately found an outdoor café at which to grab a quick, tasteless and expensive lunch. Pigeons meandered between our feet as hungry Germans ate *panini* and drank beer. Heimat lit another cigarette, and I wondered what she thought of me. She was beautiful and single, her big brown eyes protruding from her clear-skinned face. It was odd sitting with someone from Egypt in Italy. Never happened to me, and I felt that she did not trust me because I was American. Can you blame her? I asked her about her life back home. She was agitated. She said that the fundamentalists were taking over her beloved homeland. They did not care about formal education or art, only about God. Women were mistreated, and foreign investment was waning. She said that Egypt used to be aligned with Europe, but "now we are being taken over by the Arabs." Egyptians are not Arabs, she said emphatically, in a type of English that I had trouble understanding because she often skipped words altogether. She said things like "People no education. They all day. Burn books. No nutting." I kept nodding my head.

"Bank leave Egypt. People find no work. Smart people leave. Only religion. Very bad, very bad." She was totally demoralized.

"It is very bad in the United States too," I said. "People are starving in our cities, living on the streets, while millionaires become billionaires. Greed is ruling America."

She shook her head, and I was glad that I did not need to argue this point with her as I often had to at home.

"People not go to school. Home and pray. Wear," and she made a gesture, which is a mask women wear. "I not wear." I nodded as our *panini* and Cokes were served to us. They looked dry and dreadful. Mine was vegetarian, which meant tomatoes, cheese and a piece of slimy lettuce. Heimmat's was breaded chicken and looked infinitely more appealing, though from her reaction after the first bite, it was not.

"People live the streets. No money. Not care. President do nutting. Afraid of them. Very bad, very bad."

I stopped feeling sorry for myself for the time being and imagined what her life was like in a small city outside Cairo. She had a garden and a big house, and she said that her mother visited every weekend. "I work as a journalist and I am an artist."

"Artist?" My level of interest increased, if that was possible. "What do you do?"

"I am a painter."

"Really?"

She pulled out a card that read "Heimmat Jourid, journalist and artist." On it was an Egyptian landscape, with a woman carrying a jug of water.

"This is marvelous," I said truthfully.

"Thank you. I show in Venice. Susanna organize for me."

I paused, wanting to help my new friend. "Perhaps you could come to my college and show your work in our gallery? I might be able to help you with that," I volunteered.

Her eyes stood out even more. "I'll send you my dossier." I had brightened her day and was happier myself.

We stuffed down our sandwiches, which was a good thing because all that walking in Venice was making me lose weight—even though I was not skipping any meals.

We paid our check and said *arrivederci*, and I continued my trek to the Marciana. I suppose you can guess that it was around three by the time I arrived. I had stopped in this and that church, this and that bookstore and had to go to the bathroom in a pizza self-service place. The Marciana was closed when I got there. Strike. The librarians were on strike that day. Who knew? How would one know? Sullenly I walked over to a local bookstore and looked for a better guidebook. I needed something better than this American "Cheap Outings in Europe," which I had found in my apartment. Wanting to know about each of the paintings and sculptures I had seen in the churches, I bought a red, thick Italian book with no pictures, only a few sketches. Expensive and authoritative, it would help me pass the rest of the afternoon.

I walked to the Church of Santa Lucia to see the art. To my great happiness, the church contained the desiccated remains of the saint herself. I waited in line as it wound its way behind the altar to her body. Believers kissed the glass. Gawkers took surreptitious pictures. I knew this was going to be good. Dried up Medieval folks are short, was my first reaction. She must have been three feet tall. Her feet protruded out from the clothes they had wrapped her in. Her skin was tan colored, covering her bones. Her eyes stared comfortably into space and her long hair covered her arms. I wonder if it bothered her that people came to see her in that state every day. Perhaps she was proud of her looks and like a despondent mother with no time to put on her makeup for an early dinner arrival, she was mortified.

Mortified. She was certainly very dead. I made that joke in my head. Ha Ha.

The woman in front of me kissed her hand and then kissed Santa Lucia's glass enclosure. Santa Lucia could heal sick folks, and a little bit for me wouldn't be the worst thing. I wasn't that sick: I still ate and slept, but I felt as if I were carrying an elephant on my shoulders, which got off only when I was drunk. I walked into the ambulatory and bought a postcard of Saint Lucy to keep as a good luck charm, with my Chinese fortune cookie fortunes. They kept telling me my life would look up and I would be showered with gifts, and old friends would come back into my life, and I would find happiness in my work. When? What is the statute of limitations for fortune cookies?

I left the church and entered the now-rainy street with no umbrella. Damn it. It was close to dinnertime and I had to scavenge for food again. I bought some olives and salty little fish, and a piece of bread from the market, made it home and turned on the tube. Another day of my dreamy sabbatical was over.

The "Tiziano" train left at noon the next day, and I found my reserved seat right away. The new Italian trains, which look like bullet trains but run like pizzas, were perfect for the business and tourist travelers who had three or more hours to kill before having to be anywhere. Actually, that could only mean Italian business people. Florence was three and a half hours away, Rome six. And that was if there were no delays, which today might not be the case because the unending rain had brought floods to the Alpine valleys and the Po river. The Po traverses the entire peninsula and usually looks anemic. With the week of rain it was engorged, and our train was supposed to cross it somewhere south of Rovigo, near Ferrara. The conductors did

not warn us about any problem, even though all trains to Paris
had been cancelled. Sorry.

Happily, my seat was facing in the direction the train was
going, so I did not have to experience that strange eye movement
when your eyes keep readjusting themselves as you look out
at the scenery. Because, though I had a book or two to read,
I knew I wouldn't. I had the talent to daydream for hours
on end, write endlessly in my diary about how awful I was
feeling during the gift of sabbatical. A gift that few people ever
experience in a lifetime.

I sat down and thanked my lucky stars that the annoyingly
loud couple from Rome was sitting three rows ahead of me with
their naughty little daughter. They admonished her for running
down the hallway for about four hours. The little girl played
with little plastic beads an American woman was stringing
together. The woman, who spoke no Italian but seemed very
patient sitting across from her daughter, gave the girl the
beads to hold. The girl did not immediately toss them all over
the train car. Instead, she looked at them intently and after
intentionally dropping one, did her best to find it. She crawled
under people's legs and found others to help her retrieve the
plastic treasure. The parents said that she was a *terrorista*, a
word easily understood in English. She seemed like an angel to
me. They never struck her; they cajoled her in typical Italian
fashion through sarcastic remarks, which were cutting, and
awfully witty. I thought the girl was divine, truly. She loved
those little beads. She loved the little American lady who was
so patient with her.

We finally arrived in Bologna, where a new crowd of
people boarded the train. They seemed Italian corporate chic.
The men who sat down in front of me wore bright leather
shoes and tweed jackets. Their hair was black and gray, their

eyeglasses obviously designer steel rims, when we Americans were still wearing rimless. They each read the daily Italian sports newspaper, printed on pink paper. Can you imagine an American jock reading anything on pink paper? They got up to smoke a cigarette in between cars, where it was still permitted. I took the occasion to notice that my nose had begun to run uncontrollably. Within the next fifteen minutes my throat got dry and I experienced a dull headache.

Soon we arrived in Prato, the town just northwest of Florence. We had traversed the Apennines, and for the first time in two weeks, since Barb had left, the sun was resplendent in the sky, beating down on all the cars and shining all over the place. It looked hot out there too, stifling. I continued to blow my nose and skim Giorgio Bassani's *Garden of the Finzi Contini*, the story of Italian Jews in Ferrara who were sent to a concentration camp near the end of the war. It was tough reading, with many words I did not recognize, but I could enjoy the main plot, without getting too wrapped up in the details. Details were vivid, and forced plot twists unheard of, in this true-story novel. Italian writing speaks to me for its honesty.

The train stopped at Firenze Rifredi, a grimy part of Florence, and several Japanese tourists asked me if this was Florence. I said yes and no. It was not the downtown stop. That was Firenze Santa Maria Novella. My blood began to get warmer as I said those words, wanting desperately to see the terra cotta glamour of Florence in the autumn, a time that I had been in Italy only as a young girl. I remember the excitement of living in Italy for an entire year, rather than just the summer. Of collecting soccer players' cards and pasting them into my World Cup commemorative book at the beginning of the season. My cellphone rang, and a deep baritone voice asked me where I was. "Rifredi" I said, sniffling. "I vill meet you on zhe tracks," Miriam said and hung up. What joy! Quelle joie! I waxed French for a moment. French seemed right for exultation. Not that I knew very much of it.

I went back to my seat, gathered my diary and bag, and moved back into the corridor. Italians always jumped out of their seats close to their destinations, even in airplanes, where it's prohibited. My mother was the master. She was always the first in line, pushing everyone out of the way with no guilt or sense of embarrassment. The train pulled slowly into the station, and unlike Bologna's, the Florence station was set up so that the train had to pull into it and back out of it. I jumped down the steep steps off the car (after helping an elderly lady with her bags), set down my rollie bag, and looked up. Miriam was standing next to me with open arms, in a cotton pink sweater and white pants. "It's zo hot," she said, hugging me. "How strange."

This was the first sun I had felt in a while, and I pulled off my bulky pile sweater and let the warmth touch my arms. She grabbed my bag and said that we were going to Porciano, if I didn't mind, because she had to look after her mother, who wasn't well. "Wonderful," I said and coughed.

"You have a cold?" Miriam asked.

"Yes, it just came over me in the train. It must have been all that cold weather in Feltre." I told her a little bit about Antonio. She smiled, and I thought that they would make an interesting couple, given that they were both single. But Antonio, though nice, talked too much. And I have repeated this too many times.

We scrambled past all the zigzagging tourists and their wheelies and the Italians on their *telefonini*. Miriam had found a spot at a meter near the station. She threw my things in the back seat and opened the door for me.

"To, tell me more," she insisted. You know what has happened in the last couple of weeks, so no need to repeat it. I didn't lie to Miriam, or embellish any of the stories for her, though sometimes I do that so people will think I had a better time than I really did.

"How is your mother?"

"She is veak." While her English was perfect, no one spoke it quite like she did.

"I am sorry to hear that."

"Her left leg von't move. She has trouble getting out of bed. She lives in zhat cold house, vizh no one around. I vorry about her."

"How old is she now?"

"Almost ninety. She insists that she vants to pass the vinter in Berlin vith her old cousin. Ve vill have to see how she feels."

"I've never heard you worry about her before."

"She has never been sick before in her whole life." We were slaloming through traffic on one of those hectic tree-lined avenues that circumvent Florence. Miriam was tired of Florence and said, "I don't know how much longer I can take zhis. The city has changed zo much in zhe last few years. Italians have moved into the zuburbs. Florence is overrun by American tourists. Zhey have taken over zhe *centro*. You can't find any Italians in restaurants anymore." She sounded honestly hostile.

"How is your apartment?"

"Fine. I zhink you vere zhere last just after the renovations. Fine. It's noizy. Zey opened two late-night cafés across zhe street. Kids hang out in zhe streets."

Miriam was weighed down by life's problems. I felt sorry for her and happy that she was talking to me. I responded to her in Italian, because I needed to practice, but she went right on talking to me in her strange English. We made our way onto the Fi-Pi-Li, or Firenze-Pisa-Livorno *superstrada* (highway). One of the few free highways in Italy, it went due west along the Arno. My mother had gotten stuck on it one day while driving into Florence. The highway's most salient feature is that it has absolutely no shoulder. She waited in her car for what seemed hours—no one stopped to help her, so she got out and began to walk! She was nearly sideswiped three times, and her dress was drenched in mud. Finally a young Italian truck driver stopped and gave her a lift into Florence to meet Dad. The next day she bought the cellphone I have been using in Venice. Miriam had heard the whole story before.

After a few kilometers of industrial landscape and department stores, the Fi-Pi-Li wound its way through Lastra a Signa, a gorgeous town of Chianti grapes and luscious olive groves. Soon we passed Montelupo, the home of wholesale Italian ceramics. Miriam asked me about my job and I found myself, for the first time, recounting to her the details of my tenure battle. I told her that the president of the college, who was a "friend" of my family, told me during my final meeting with him, when I had a pen and pad in my hands ready to take down any notes (as my lawyer had instructed, should we sue), that my father was a terrible person, that I was much more talented than he, and would go farther, and that my mother, like my father, was self-involved and out of it.

"Vhy did he do zhat?" She seemed sad and puzzled.

"Because Dad had written him a scathing email appealing to justice when he heard that the school was trying to fuck up my tenure. The president got pissed off and dumped it on me. I was in tears in his office. Broken down from stress and this verbal assault on my parents. Then he said that he wanted to be my mentor and that he would protect me from now on. He stood up, said congratulations, and pulled me to his waist. Ugh."

"How beezarre."

My hands began to sweat and I got sick to my stomach. I had made a pact with myself not to talk about the tenure battle or my college when not necessary. The injustices, after all, are boring. It's like listening to a child whine about ice cream she doesn't like.

"I never told Mom or Dad the story."

"Zhat's probably a good idea. Zhey don't need to know."

Miriam got off the Fi-Pi-Li at Empoli, a busy town smack between Pisa and Florence. It was known for its flourishing computer-tech industry. We drove through town until we hit a red light, with a long line of cars before it. We waited and waited until everyone in line began honking at the same time. The light turned green. Making a sharp right, we crossed a long bridge over the Arno River. In Empoli, the banks of the river were lined with garbage. A man in a rowboat fished.

After driving a few kilometers, Miriam said that we had to stop at a lighting store because she wanted to get her German cousin, the one who had promised to take care of her mother, a new designer lamp. We pulled over and went into a store that was like the Gucci for lights. It felt like a tanning salon inside, with all those light bulbs. Miriam was drawn to the seventies look, square and severe. She found it immediately and called for the salesman. Feeling rather sick and sniffling, I walked outside and pulled out my cellphone to call Barb and tell her that I had arrived in Florence, without a hitch. Her phone was busy, so I left a message, and was glad that I had completed this duty before Miriam was ready. She was always impatient with me when I spoke to Barb on the phone. I walked in to find her shaking her head at the high prices and telling the salesperson that she would not return.

"Zhis is outrageous," she said, motioning me to get back into the car so we could stop at the supermarket to buy some groceries. I felt excited to be with her, and scared that I was doing everything wrong. Do you know anyone like that? We stopped at the COOP, a ubiquitous store in Italy and bought dinner. Miriam found a cart and charged into the store, her silk scarf trailing her. She asked me what I wanted ten times, as if I were a child, and then checked a couple of more times. "Zucchini all right? Are you sure? Beans? Do you eat beans? Bread? Do you like zhis one?" I loved it all, as long as it wasn't meat, I assured her. Anyway, this is Italy—what's not to like?

We got a little number from the machine and waited to place our deli order. It seemed as if the ladies behind the counter were deliberately skipping Miriam. Miriam finally piped up in her Italian with a German accent, with great exuberance and charm, waving her arms like an Italian and demanding a bit of this cheese, a little of that fish salad, a dollop of artichoke spread, a little bean salad, and some Pecorino cheese. The woman did not return her warmth, and I wondered if Miriam was hurt by this. She just grabbed the containers in both hands and plopped them in our basket, with no comment. We bought some Pasta Barilla (Ma says it's the best) and made our way to the busy check-out line. Italians never said *Buon giorno* (good day) or *Buona sera* (good evening) to me in Venice and they didn't here in Empoli either. Big deal. At least I wasn't alone and had some good food that Miriam insisted on paying for. Being alone was something I needed to deal with, so my parents insisted.

Miriam stuck the food in the trunk of her car and opened the door for me. She did things a little bit like a man, or a pushy mother. I liked driving with her because she drove fast and was completely secure with what she was doing, passing slower cars or going through red lights (everybody does that). She even had a photo of the two of us taken by the police. She said it was a good thing that I was with her, or else she would have been going even faster. We took the road toward Vinci, in a northwesterly direction. It was so warm out that I opened the car window halfway without sneezing. Miriam said that she had done a little more work on her apartment, fixed the stove and second-floor sink. She had bought a new washer, and I asked her if I could do a load.

"Vhat do you zhink it's for?"

We drove passed Vinci—of Leonardo of—and towards Lamporecchio, of the famous Boccaccio story of Day III of his *Decameron*. In this story, the naughty nuns of Lamporecchio invite a "deaf, dumb and blind man" to work at the nunnery and then have sex with him, thinking that he can't divulge their secrets. But he is faking it and tells the truth in the end because he is so tired of satisfying all the nuns. Boccaccio wrote his hundred stories to entertain and educate women, who in medieval and Renaissance times were not allowed to receive degrees at the university. To show their gratitude to Boccaccio, many later women writers wrote stories imitating Boccaccio's salty tales. I've written a parody of the story, which I included in my book *Fiammetta*. The mention of my story serves to mark the middle of this novel and to prepare the reader for the climax.

You may wish to get something to eat here.

Miriam and I drove into town, and rather quickly, up a narrow, steep, and winding road that skirted olive groves and small villas. She did not slow down at the curves, which brought me great joy as I was swung left and right by the force. My sneezing commenced again as soon as we pulled into her little courtyard. I found a wet tissue deep in my pockets and blew.

She said she was sorry that I had a cold, but that we would go see her mother, and that perhaps she could do something about it. Then she said, "Vhat do you expect, riding around vizh zhe vindow open."

I got my stuff out of the trunk and she brought in the groceries. I hadn't been in her house for years, and to my great relief it was just as beautifully unkempt as I had remembered. She put the groceries on the kitchen table and turned on some lights. It was about six in the evening, and the sun would be setting soon. Putting a few things into the refrigerator, she asked me if I wouldn't mind some tea.

"Yes, yes. That would make my throat feel a little better."

"Here, and take zhis aspirin. She plopped two effervescent aspirin in a glass of mineral water. "Drink zhis." Unlike some naturopaths in Pennsylvania I knew, Miriam did not think of aspirin as an abomination. She asked me how my sabbatical was going, and I told her it was going well, even though I was mysteriously depressed. "Can I borrow your computer out here?" I asked.

"Of course, but I already told you zhat." She was obviously tenser than usual. She threw the vegetables into the refrigerator and called her mother on her cellphone. They spoke in Italian and she said, "We'll be right over."

She hung up and said that she had prepared some beef stew for her mother and wanted to bring it over now. I was really anxious to see Maria again. I loved her because she had spent her entire life trying to make people feel better. We took an umbrella and walked out the door onto a narrow, paved road. On one side, facing the valley, there was a steep drop-off into an olive grove, and on the other side an old rock wall, dilapidated, holding up the other side of the mountain. Water followed us down the road underneath our sneakers. Maria lived in a tiny apartment some two hundred yards away. Cars with German license plates filled the tiny parking lot in front of her garden. She heard us arriving and opened the door. Maria was small and frail, her straight white hair and translucent skin more delicate than I could have imagined. She was bundled up in layers of blue sweaters and wearing gloves. Miriam spoke to her in a loud voice, with the intonation of a famous opera singer.

"Mozzer, it is so cold in here. Vhy don't you turn up zhe heat?" Miriam walked to the thermostat. "Ten centigrade!"

"That's plenty warm for me," Maria responded quietly. She had much less of an accent—barely detectable. "So good to see you, Jean." She came toward me, but I asked her not to touch me because I had a cold.

"True." She paused. "Can I help you, my dear?"

"I'm fine," I assured her. "It's damp in that Venice apartment."

"Vhat did you expect?" Miriam interjected. "She does not take care of herself." Miriam was really in a bad way, I thought.

Maria asked Miriam to look up her "code" in her little black book and tell her what the numbers were. Miriam complied and said "320." Maria instructed me to place my right palm on a brass round platform that had two wires coming out of it and was attached to a rectangular box with three knobs. Maria set the knobs to the numbers Miriam had dictated and told me to hold my hand there until she said to lift it. I hoped that perhaps Maria had some of that magical tea she had promised me the last time I visited. It was for self-esteem problems. After about fifteen seconds she told me to lift my hand and said I would feel better soon. How soon? She did not say. But I believed her. (During my tenure troubles at my college, Miriam's mother used a crystal dangling from a string to determine my future. She said that a woman would help me. In fact, the mean female dean did begrudgingly give the go-ahead for my tenure appointment.) Maria pulled out the crystal again and watched it sway back and forth a couple of times. Then she put it back into her pocket. I wondered what it said. Miriam asked if she would like her to heat the stew, and Maria said, "No, I will do it myself." Small, ancient cards lay on her kitchen table. We had interrupted her complex game of solitaire. Witches need a lot of alone time, I thought. Solitaire was perfect.

Miriam made her mother's bed and cleaned a few dishes. She wiped off the counter and put a few clothes away. After pulling a broom from the closet, she gave the floor a quick go over, never moving a chair out of the way, carefully navigating around a small piece of carpet. She asked her mother if she needed anything at the store, and after a negative reply we left without a hug because I was still sick.

Back home, Miriam pulled out our goodies, and it was so warm that we ate out on the veranda, under a canopy of brown wisteria. She opened a bottle of red and poured me a glass. None for her—too fattening. The alcohol filtered quickly into my bloodstream, making the Tuscan lights that sparkled in the wet air look as if the stars had landed on the ground. I was in Tuscany with a favorite friend—how blessed. Miriam made a little pasta, and I peeled and chopped garlic for my favorite homemade sauce, *aglio, olio e peperoncino.* It is so musical: garlic, oil and flaked red peppers. We threw the meal together at the table, olives and white bean salad, cheese and my pasta. Only I had put way too much garlic in the sauce, and Miriam pushed it all to the side of her plate. Italian garlic is much more potent than American garlic. I felt bad that she didn't like my sauce, and pretended not to notice her picking out the garlic and drinking a lot of water after each bite.

"I am vorried about my mutter," she finally said.

"Yes, I can see."

"She doesn't vant to live anymore." I looked at her. Miriam had never spoken so honestly to me before. She never admitted her vulnerability. "She von't go to a doctor for her leg."

"What will you do?"

"Zere is nozzing I can do. She vill not listen. She vill only see Dante. 'Dante vill take care of me.'"

"Who is Dante?"

"A healer."

"I see."

"Jean." She stopped. "I have no ozzer family besides my mutter. Ven she goes, I vill be alone," and tears began to form on her cheeks, salty tears, for the first time. I reached across and held her hand, wanting her to continue talking but not knowing what to say to be supportive. Miriam was my Italian life's idol. She was in pain.

"Would you like a tissue?" How lame. Why do lame things come out when you want to show how much you love a person? I reached for the shopping bag that had a plastic sack of fresh tissues. "Here, I haven't touched this," I said as I passed it to her. She blew her nose and tried to stop the tears, but they kept flowing.

"She is zhe center of my life, my teacher," she continued.

"I am sorry. What do you think is the matter with her leg?"

"Arzritis."

"Can you die from that?" I asked.

"She vants to die. She vill make herself die. She is not afraid of ze ozzer zide. She has been zhere before. She is just tired of life and vill not seek help. Zo stubborn."

"Maybe she will live for you," I thought, a strong intuition stirring my heart.

"No, it is over," Miriam was inconsolable. The tears flowed.

We finished our dinner and I washed the dishes in the sink. She showed me my bedroom on the second floor with the bath next to it and gave me some towels and another aspirin. "Take zhis, you vill feel better." For a witch, she was sure pushing the drugs. Miriam used astral powers to heal her clients all over the world, some suffering from cancer and arthritis. She stayed up at night and spoke softly to the starts. Sometimes she spoke to a real bigwig like Galileo or Leonardo. They helped her figure out problems. She had healed the arthritis in my mother's hands.

I went into the narrow bathroom to brush my teeth and wash my face. Hundreds of flies were buzzing about. She must have left the window open, which looks out into the splendid countryside. I reached across the shower and shut it, as flies circled me. Trying not to focus on them, I brushed my teeth with a little *Pasta del Capitano,* the Italian Crest, a traditional but not particularly sweetened brand of toothpaste. In the mirror, I saw a contented face with little red rings around the nostrils from blowing. My hair was clean and pulled into a ponytail, eyebrows dark and full, my brown eyes radiant despite my cold. I changed into my flannel pajamas and walked into the bedroom with a pile of dirty clothes. I'll be so happy when these jeans are finally washed, I thought. I'd been wearing them on and off without a wash for two weeks. They were the only pants that didn't make the inside of my thighs red after long walks in Venice. I pulled out the *Garden of the Finzi-Contini* and read a few pages, until my eyes were almost shut. After turning off the light, I looked up at the ceiling, counted all the corners of the room and made a wish. "I wish that Miriam does not suffer too much about her mother. And let Maria get well." I drifted to sleep.

When I woke up, I heard the rain beating on the shutters

of my window. Birds were chirping and someone was saying goodbye to Miriam outside my window. A car started and I heard it back out the driveway and leave. Miriam came back inside. I changed into my clothes and walked downstairs to see Miriam and see how she was feeling. My cold had subsided, and I was sniffling only a little. Miriam had breakfast already prepared for me, at nine, which is what the kitchen clock read.

"How are you feeling, my dear?" she asked me in English, and as was customary between us, I answered in Italian,

"Better."

"Tea?"

"Yes."

"Vith lemon?"

"Yes."

We sat and talked for a bit until she said she was going to check on her mother and would be back in an hour.

"Who was that in the yard this morning?" I asked.

"Fulvio."

"Your old boyfriend?"

"Yes."

Miriam had been his mistress for fifteen years. One day about a year ago, Fulvio told his wife about Miriam and everything fell apart. Miriam said the wife went nuts and threatened to harm herself if the affair didn't stop. She believed her and cut it off. Miriam was left, as many mistresses are, relieved and desperate for attention. She told me that he was a great lover. Insecurity does not dampen with age; it gets passively more insidious. Miriam said that the wife was on sedatives and sleeping pills. Fulvio still came by to help her pick the olives every late fall, and he was here to prepare for next weekend's marathon picking session.

"I am glad that you are still friends," I said.

"Me too." Miriam was definitely less edgy this morning. "Listen, let's go for a valk vhen I get back. I'll show you zhis beautiful church on zhe hill vhere my cousin from Los Angeles got married a couple of years ago."

"Sounds good. I'll take a shower."

"See you zoon," and she was gone.

I washed myself in her narrow shower and was relieved to find that the flies there were sleeping. I was careful not to step on any and not to disturb them, so they wouldn't wake up and bother me.

Miriam was back in an hour on the dot, and we found two umbrellas just in case the torrential rains returned during our walk across the Tuscan mountainside. We walked down a narrow path into the little town of Porciano. It had only one major road running through it and was particularly empty this rainy morning. Miriam said the church was just down a path on the left. We marveled at all the new construction that was taking place around us. Old villas were being stripped down to their foundations and new ones built on top. Old ladies said cheery hellos to us as their little dogs trailed them. The church was on a small promontory overlooking the town of Lamporecchio. It was flanked by a grassy piazza, and Miriam walked right up to the door. She shook her head, "It's closed. It's zo lovely inside."

She told me where the bride and groom had stood for pictures and where they had set up tables and chairs for their outdoor lunch after the ceremony. The church was built in the seventeenth century and was modest from the outside. There was a little cemetery in front. "Zometimes I zhink that I vant to buried here," Miriam said. "Zometimes, I don't know vhere my true home is."

Miriam was born in Italy to German parents and spent

her early years in Stuttgart, dressed as a boy. She was still masculine, in a kind of German way, but very feminine to me in that masculine kind of way. I loved her. Miriam wanted to show me the land she had bought a couple of years ago from an old farmer and pointed to a spot on the hill to our right.

"I'd love to see it."

"Zometimes I zhink zhat I made a mistake. Zhere is a lot of upkeep, you'll zee," she warned me.

We walked back across the busy street to a narrow, snaky, unpaved road that went up the mountain. Miriam said that at the time she had needed something to call her own, besides her friendly spirits, something more earthly. Drippy olive trees stuffed with black olives ready to be picked accompanied our slow ascent. After crossing a little stream, Miriam pointed around us and said that this was her land, about an acre. We walked by a messy grapevine and Miriam pulled off a white bunch, asking me if I wanted to taste the sweetness, because she was not about to. Of course I ate a couple. They tasted like sugar balls. "Wonderful." I began to feel more at ease with my dear friend and suddenly I remembered.

"Miriam—" I paused. "I have begun seeing ghosts in the last year."

She stopped in her tracks, dropped the remaining grapes and looked me in the eye. "Really," and the tone of her voice descended. "Vhere?"

"In the cemetery. I ride my bicycle through it every day to get to school."

"Vhat time of day?"

"The morning."

"Are zhey men or women?"

"Both."

"Do you zee all of zhem?"

"Yes."

"Vhat do zhey look like?"

"Regular people. Am I going crazy?"

"Not at all. Can you zee any now?"

"I haven't been looking."

"Zhink hard."

I paused and thought and waited. Nothing came.

She smiled a huge smile, the first I had seen in a while. We continued our walk through the olive grove, occasionally stopping to look at a flowering plant or to pick up another piece of fruit that had been lying on the ground. Miriam picked up a pear. We saw lizards scatter as we walked on a narrow path, and I pointed out the *ortica* (stinging nettle) plant that used to hurt me and cause itchy skin when I was in Italy as a child. "Made into a tea, ortica is excellent for people who are losing their hair," Miriam reminded me. We noticed the thick, prickly grass growing between the rocks of an ancient wall and the scent of the wet leaves in the air. When it rains hard in Tuscany, the hillsides get saturated and the water begins to stream down the mountain: it hadn't gotten to that point yet today. The electricity goes dead when the rains hit, and Tuscans spend many afternoons in the dark. Miriam showed me the path that led to the top of the mountain and said that she would take me there another day, it was too wet now.

We saw enormous mushrooms in the fields—edible, Miriam said—called *ombrelloni* (beach umbrellas). I wanted to pick some and sauté them in white wine, but Miriam said she had never tried picking them before and was a little wary of mushrooms anyway. We saw bulbous, bright white mushrooms and blackberries still on the vine. Walnut trees had released their crops, and we picked some up. Fig and plum trees were resting for the new season. While walking through this field, we could have feasted on earth's delicacies without ever going to the store, as if we were eating from the fanciest gourmet shop, but in a much better atmosphere. We heard a dog bark before us and knew that we had reached the gates of paradise.

Chapter 7

When we returned to Miriam's apartment, she picked up the phone and made appointments for us to have pedicures with her friend Silvana. Silvana and her daughter Paola owned the beauty salon "Da Paola" in Lamporecchio, and Paola would give us each a foot massage while the other waited. Miriam drove fast down the steep mountain until an old man driving a clunker at thirty kilometers an hour was suddenly in front of her. She began to scream, "Vhy today? Vhere are you going old man?" Who said witches had to be patient people? Once in town we found a spot and jumped out. I let Miriam go in first and followed her to the back of the store, past the hair salon, where several male customers were getting a haircut from Silvana's husband.

"Ciao, Luigi!" Miriam belted out.

"Buona sera signorine," he replied. "Silvana waits for you in the back."

Silvana was busy putting the finishing touches on the nails of a pretty woman. She stopped to say hello and introduced the woman as "Indira's daughter." She knew my mother, who got her toes done here too. Once you have tried Silvana, you can never go to anyone else. Not even a boutique in Florence, my mother told me. Silvana marveled that my Italian was so good. "She sounds Italian," she said, smiling and putting the final coat of paint on her client's toenails. Silvana was about sixty, rotund, small and short-haired. She had blue eyes and a long smile. "I will be with you in a moment."

We sat down and fumbled through glamour magazines until we heard Paola telling Miriam to come downstairs, she would start with her. Miriam looked psyched and I waited for Silvana to finish. It wasn't but a few minutes. I had never had anything done to my body, except a haircut, and Mamma usually did that. Pampering seemed out of my league. Not naturally drawn to pedicures (I refused the manicure because someone could see it), I took off my socks and sneakers, hoping that my feet were not too smelly, as they are known to be. Silvana said that my feet were unusually soft, as were my hands. It's a weird collagen problem. And I have never done manual labor or walked much barefoot. She soaked my feet in soapy water and asked me how my mother was doing. Fine. I hadn't thought about her too much in the last couple of weeks. She liked living in New York and was enjoying her retirement, going to the movies with her friend Barba and bragging about getting the senior citizen discount.

I asked Silvana where she grew up, and she said near Arezzo—she was Tuscan by birth. She had married her husband when she was twenty-four and moved to Lamporecchio to start the business. They loved it here. She pulled my left foot out of the water and patted it dry. She continued to talk about her childhood, and her beloved father, who after the death of her mother mourned for ten years before finding a new wife. Seemed anomalous, given that most Italian men have mistresses anyway. He was a good man, she repeated again and again. Especially after he beat up her sister's boyfriend, who had been beating her sister for a year. Her father died after never taking a day off from work. Like Michelangelo, she said. Did you know that Michelangelo went to sleep with his shoes on so that he would not waste time the next morning putting them on? While

Italians might have reputations for not working, many work very hard, famous ones included.

Silvana began to gently clean the toe stuff off my feet, and I felt bad that some of that stuff was spraying onto her sweater. She took a closer look at this growth on my big toe, which she said was a *fungo*, which sounds like a mushroom, but is a fungus. It was eating away at my big toe's toenail like rust. She cleaned it off and recommended some drops that cost a lot of money at the pharmacy next door—but all her clients are satisfied with the product. She wrote down the name on a little piece of paper, which I would lose, like all the other pieces of paper with important things on them. She said that Mom had told her about my tenure stress the year before. "Your mother was so worried about you," she said sincerely. "She said that they were trying to take your job. I knew it would never happen, that you are too smart, *signorina*." I was honored to know that people in Italy were rooting for me. After cleaning my toes and shaving off some old skin from the heel and the bottoms of my feet, she asked me what shade of nail polish I desired.

"Copper," I said without hesitating. "That's what Miriam is wearing, and I want to wear the same."

"It's a lovely shade. Makes her feet look younger."

With the expertise of Leonardo, she applied two coats of paint to my toenails and said that we were done. She told me she gave the best pedicure in the region—she was expert in the area of feet. She said that they should dry for ten minutes or so and I should sit still while she cleaned up and prepared for Miriam. I told her a bit about my students in Pennsylvania, about a thesis one was writing about a British woman musician. Silvana called down to Paola to see if we had enough time to get a cappuccino. "I would like to offer you a coffee," she said to me. "You are a sensitive girl."

I couldn't refuse, even though I don't drink coffee, never did, so I put my sweat socks back on and my shoes, and we walked down the street to the local café. Silvana ordered a cappuccino and I had a Coke, so "American," they must have been thinking. Why drink Coke when you can have coffee? I don't know. Coffee just grosses me out the door.

We stood at the counter and Silvana smiled and smiled and looked at me intently. She loved me for some odd reason. I told her that I wrote about women in history and that my next project would be about the Paduan noblewoman. She smiled and smiled and her eyes sparkled, as if marveling at a favorite granddaughter—only I was forty and not related to her at all. She told me that Paola was engaged to a man Miriam did not like. In fact, no one liked him. He worked for a big pots-and-pans company and helped set up showrooms at trade shows. He was rarely around and had an unsympathetic air about him. Handsome, though, you couldn't argue with that. I told her how much I liked the computer guy across the street. He had let me use his Internet connection for nothing, when my computer died. And handsome too.

I slugged down the rest of my Coke like an Italian coffee, it hurt my throat, and we walked back to the salon for the *pièce de resistance*—the foot massage from Paola. Miriam was busy chatting with Paola upstairs and when she saw us reappear, she began raving about the most heavenly foot massage. "Heaven," she repeated as she took her place in Silvana's office, ready to get her feet pampered some more. Paola said to follow her downstairs, she was ready for me. Paola's little spa was gorgeous. Tuscan tiles lined the floors; little pencil drawings filled the walls. It was really clean. No carpet. No dust. She told me to lie down on the table and that she would adjust it to make it longer, because I was tall. I felt a little manly in Italy, more so than in, say, Vermont, because I was taller than most girls, and more *robusta*. The vestige of playing basketball.

Paola was trained in holistic medicine and massage and took only herbs for her ailments, which, after I lay down, she said were numerous. The one she wanted to speak most about was her migraines. They were brutal. She said she cut out eggs and cheese and chocolate and chicken, and meat in general. That's a good thing. "Do you get the aura?" I asked, a recovering migraine sufferer, especially during those excruciating days of working at Fiat in New York City. Going shopping at Macy's with my mother triggered them too. Was it the fluorescent lights or my mother's nagging? I don't know, they were both distant memories. I felt terrible that Paola was in so much pain. She should stop rubbing people's feet and begin getting her boyfriend to rub hers. Maybe the anxieties over the boyfriend were manifesting themselves in her head. She wasn't in love with him, just thought she was. Her head ached from the thoughts. At this moment, Paola was the most beautiful thing in the world. She cared deeply for my feet and also my heart.

I spent the next morning working on my presentation for the MAP convention in Tampa. The subject was sensitivity to gay, lesbian, bi-sexual, and transgender college athletes. Sports. I had stopped now, but was very active in college. Getting close to forty, my body just didn't feel like playing competitively anymore. I couldn't keep up with the younger players, who ran circles and hemispheres around me. My body ached after a brief sprint to chase my dog when he got out of the house. Mostly, my ego hurt because I wasn't that good anymore. All style, no substance. I was the wily veteran with no more verve. So I walked my dog a lot and rode my bicycle to school, to avoid paying the university parking fees, which added up to the raise I got after tenure. My sports memories consisted of just that, and they were from years ago.

But I had gotten interested in a new issue, an issue that I could kick some butt with: the suffering of closeted athletes in college. I remember being so scared that someone in college would figure out that I was bi-sexual that I refused to shower with the team, and I didn't sleep when I was in bed with my teammate Lisa Pares, because she wore this little slinky, cleavage-showing nighty. We had to share a bed to save money, and they put four in a hotel room on away trips. It was torture because I did not understand what I was feeling. Only that I wanted it to stop. And it did, once Lisa seduced me after the season was over in her little dorm room at Vassar College. Then we got tired of each other and she graduated.

In the meantime, I could not go talk to my coach, who was soooo gay but said that her boyfriend never came to our games because he worked nights in a bank—she was afraid to lose her job. And our assistant coach was sleeping with the star forward, but they sneaked in and out of the math library so as not to be seen. Who would ever study there? The bottom line is that a few students had come to me at Mead College to say that they had been harassed by others because they were gay. One time it happened in the locker room and once in the training room. Both involved the words "faggot." I also overheard a member of the college's b-ball team at a game call an opposing player a "dyke." This had to stop, and so I met with the dean of students and anyone else who would listen to me. I am on a crusade now. My first mission is to give this paper about the effects of this kind of prejudice on the welfare of student athletes. I ought to know. I barely made it out of college alive. Good thing my liver is unusually adroit at breaking down alcohol and Quaaludes.

I began typing my paper into Miriam's old IBM, first a little about my own experience and those of students I had spoken to, then a little about what professors can do to help their students, then a call for others to join the fight. This should fill up fifteen minutes. Not being much of an activist, I found my new role of fighting for a cause challenging. I mean, I am by nature an activist, just not in a particularly activist way. I fight for what I think is right—by rules that I feel in my heart—and I make people mad in the process. How confusing. I wrote the first draft in one big push and stopped to get some more tea. My cold had pretty much vanished, and the tea soothed the last vestiges of its symptoms. Miriam opened the door and asked me how it was going, to which I responded fine and asked how her mother was.

"Not good." She looked very concerned.

"Her leg still hurt?"

"Yes, Dante is coming by zhis afternoon to look at it. He is zhe only wone whom she vill allow to help her."

I had heard a little about Dante in the past. He was Miriam's best friend, a Tuscan psychologist who works with inmates. She asked me if I needed to print my stuff and I said yes, it was only five pages long. Miriam hooked up the printer, which took five minutes to load, and printed my paper for me. I was thrilled. How lucky I am to have such a devoted friend. I told her a little about the paper. She did not seem particularly interested. Sex stuff belonged in the closet for Miriam, or at late night parties and naughty soirees. Not school. We disagreed here—since I could not separate school from the real world, and neither could most people.

We heard a knock on the door and saw it open. "Ciao, Dante."

A beautiful, short, dark-skinned man walked in. His head

was shaved and he had a pointy nose and long eyelashes. He was out of breath because he had ridden his bicycle over the hills from Prato. Miriam asked him if he wanted some coffee. "Of course, would or could I ever say no?"

Miriam introduced me to him, and we sat down in the kitchen in front of the wood fire, the same place where Miriam and I had had that important talk some ten years ago. "Distance yourself from your family," she had said. "And get a shrink." Dante found a glass of salted sunflower seeds that Miriam kept on a shelf. "Eat, eat," she said. "I know how much you like zhem." He took a handful and poured them into his mouth. I loved that he liked them so much, like a child. He sat down and began fumbling with some papers.

"Your mother is very stubborn," he said. "She needs to leave that apartment, be with more people. She is too lonely."

"I vant to take her to Germany in zhe vinter," Miriam said. "I zhink zhat she vill go."

They spoke a little more about her mother's condition and then focused on Miriam's tooth.

"How does it feel?" He asked in a sweet tone.

"Not vell."

"How long has it been?" I asked.

"Eight montzs." I was astonished. Imagine an eight-month-old toothache. "It's infected," she surmised.

"Shouldn't you take antibiotics?" I asked.

"They don't work on me."

"Why not?"

She didn't answer and smiled at Dante. Maybe they don't work on witches?

Dante began to bemoan the rain. "This is strange, I...."

Miriam interrupted his thought: "Jean, do mind if I tell Dante vhat you told me yesterday?" I looked at her, somewhat puzzled. "About the ghosts?"

"No," I said without much thought. "Go ahead."

She recounted our conversation to him. It was Sunday, October 13, at 1:34 p.m. I will never forget that day. The day the miracle happened. The day my life changed forever.

Dante listened calmly. Then he asked me the same questions: What did they look like? Where did you see them? When? He began to look at me—feel me, I could tell. He asked me about my music. I said that I play the piano, that I have played since I was eight years old.

"What do you play?" he asked.

"The usual, Brahms and Mozart and Schubert. I was never good enough to play concertos, though."

He asked me if I spoke any other languages as well as I speak Italian.

"A little French."

He shook his head.

"Listen to her!" He couldn't believe the lovely pronunciation, he said. "Musical." He continued, "Miriam has told me that you are good at sports. You won an award?"

"Yes, when I was in college, I was an All-American in basketball. Whatever that means. I was just glad to be able to play four years in college. It was my life, running and jumping."

He continued to shake his head, and for the first time in my entire life, I felt the weight of sadness, the heaviness of melancholy, the dread of despair vanish.

"Do you see ghosts all the time?" he asked.

"Only when I am looking for them. It is a little bit like a radio frequency. When I tune into them I see them, when I don't they are gone. Should I be afraid?"

"Not at all. They can help you. They can help you with your

fears and they can help you reach your goals."

"How?"

"By helping them. They want to repay you."

"How do I help them?"

"Talk to them. They are lonely and in need of comfort. Comfort them."

"How?"

"You will know how. I cannot tell you."

"People will think I'm crazy."

"Do you think that you are?"

"No."

"Don't speak about this to those who don't understand." Then he said the most beautiful words ever uttered to me. "What is, is what you sense to be true. What feels right is right. Listen to yourself—you will never go wrong."

I told him about the time I went to get a reading done from my friend Constance's seer in Pennsylvania. She told me that my third eye was too open and that I had to shut it or I would be hurt.

"Nonsense. Open, feel, breathe, live—you will be able to help many people." He smiled and ate more sunflower seeds.

I was in love, I mean, in that feeling. My heart quickened, my palms sweated, my eyes opened. My heart awoke from a sleep. Dante said what I had always known to be true—but never accepted. Somehow I had discovered the missing dimension in my life, which had always been there, like a long-lost friend or an old photograph, waiting, waiting to be revived.

"Do you see auras?" he asked me.

"I don't know."

"Lights around people?"

"I haven't noticed."

Miriam said that she saw them.

He got up and turned off the kitchen light. Sitting down, he looked at me intently and said that he saw a yellow hue above my head, like a long hat. Miriam said that she saw it too.

"Vhat do you zee around me?" Miriam asked.

"I don't know," I responded. "How should I look?"

"Look as if you vere looking behind me. It's a kind of trance, as if I do not even exist."

I tried and saw gray around Miriam, a gray field. Nothing spectacular.

"What does it mean?" I asked.

"Do not give a meaning to what you see," Dante said. "Just look."

This seemed odd. Don't so-called fortune-tellers always give things meaning? I was puzzled, but relieved. I hadn't given my ghosts much meaning. They did not seem to have any. They were not like reading a book or decoding a secret language or analyzing a piano sonata by Beethoven.

Dante urged me to see, feel, experience. Over and over he said these words—in Italian. Miriam talked a little about the woman who lived down the hill. "She's a witch. People from far avay come to zee her every Sunday. Zhere is a line around her house. But—" She paused. "She never takes money. People with a special talent such as yours should never take money."

"Why?"

"It clouds zhe truth. Anyway zhere is one good way to know vhezher she is real or not. Every Christmas gifts are piled up high in her living room."

"Maybe I should go talk to her?"

"Vhy?" Miriam said abruptly. "You don't need to know anything from her."

"I thought that maybe she could help explain what it is I am seeing," I reasoned.

"No." Dante corrected me. "The explanation is within yourself."

I never had a teacher, mother or mentor who told me to be myself. Only people who corrected me. Dante had given me the biggest gift I could have ever asked for. And it was just the beginning.

"Do you have a goal in mind when you write?" he asked me.

"Sometimes. Sometimes I want to finish a story or a novel."

"Don't," he suggested, "just write. See what comes out. Let your ideas flow freely. Write."

JUST WRITE, Dante said. God Bless You, Dante and Miriam! I loved them with all the love I could muster—and at this moment there was a lot of it.

That evening Miriam and I drove in the rain back to her apartment in Florence. I hadn't been there for ten years, just after the renovation was completed. She lived on the Via della Chiesa, around the corner from the Pitti Palace, in the thick of the Florence bustle. Instead of wasting time looking for a spot to park, Miriam paid for a parking space at about $150 a month: it wasn't that bad. We walked on the narrow sidewalk to her apartment and up four and a half flights of stairs. She lived on the top floor, in a duplex with a modern kitchen and bathroom. She asked me to take my shoes off and put on some slippers. We did not say much after that. I brushed my teeth in the little bathroom adjacent to my bedroom/study, which was adjacent to a big kitchen. Miriam pulled out the sofa chair and put down some fresh sheets and a pillowcase. Her study was lined with books about Galileo and astrology, the occult, and Florence. Her father had given her his library before he died of cancer, and she saved his collection of Italian modernist novels and histories of Italy. A picture of her father and her friend Ida, who had also died of cancer, filled a bookshelf. Miriam wished me good night, said she was exhausted and walked upstairs. *Sogni d'oro* (golden dreams), she reminded me after she turned off the kitchen light. My dreams would never be the same.

When I first moved out of New York City, where I had grown up and, as you might remember, gone to college, I had tremendous nightmares. Was it the quiet of the quaint Pennsylvania town? Being alone? I don't know. But they were about murders and falling out of planes and not getting on planes and being stranded and getting hit by planes. I would wake up in a sweat every morning. My shrink advised me that when I woke up I should try to finish the nightmares with a happy ending. So the next time I fell out of a plane, I imagined myself flying with the birds. The next time my head was chopped off by my brother, it got reconnected magically and we had a nice reconciliatory tea at the local diner, talking about how much we meant to each other. The nightmares refused to go away and became even worse, if you can imagine, and this was while I was in love with a colleague at Mead, who took me fly-fishing and was sleeping with her students. The worst one was when I dreamt that she and her former husband were standing over me about to suffocate me with a pillow. This just had to stop. He was the one, later, who tried to sabotage my tenure at the college.

I considered medication. I considered hypnosis. But the primary thing is that they did not really affect my waking life. Now it seemed to me that for the first time, my subconscious was free to run wild, free from the shackles of family and city life. Now I could move from being a graduate school peon to becoming a flourishing adult. From being Mamma's little girl to erecting some boundaries (how about three hundred miles?), no longer allowing her to call me a "gooda fo nothing" and "oogly" with a "bigga behind." I got a bell and I rang it whenever Mamma criticized me. That was her signal to stop, right now. No questions asked. But my mamma has a sense of humor, and when she could not help but say that my hair looked like a bush, she would say, "Get the bell," and then proceed with the insult. After a year or so of bell ringing, Mamma stopped insulting me. She had made a living doing that, and she stopped. Put your foot down, women. Ring the bell. One day I will go on the Oprah show with this idea. That's when I will know I have arrived.

I put my head down on the pillow and stared at the ceiling to make my wish. "I wish that Miriam, Dante, and Barb are happy." Barb. How am I going to tell Barb about the ghosts and my "talent" for seeing them? She is a loving, giving and honest person, but a straight shooter, a lawyer. Would she want to break up with me? I will wait a couple of days before telling her. Can't hurt. I looked out the window in front of me and noticed a blue glass ball hanging in the air. It twirled—and I sensed the presence of an older man in the room. He was bald and hunched over and strong and skinny. He told me that he was watching over Miriam. "I am her father."

"Nice to meet you," I said. "I can see ghosts and it's not weird."

"Not at all."

He was gone. That night I had the most deliriously happy dream. My mother came to a conference with me. She and I skateboarded around the college campus and stopped to sit on a grassy spot. I caressed her and told her that her father was fine in heaven. She looked at me lovingly. Nighty night.

Miriam prepared some breakfast for me the next morning. The tea, bread and jelly were delicious. She had just gotten off the phone with her mother and said that she was still in pain.

"I am sorry," I said.

"Vhat vill you do today?"

"I'm going to work on my sports paper, and then I have to go to the Museo dell' Opera del Duomo to see Donatello's marble *cantorie* (choir stall) for my other conference paper."

"You vill love it."

"How about you?"

"I have to vork until late tonight. I probably vont be home until eight."

"Can I make you some dinner?"

"Sure."

"I promise not to put in too much garlic. Do you like asparagus?"

"Yes."

"Tofu?"

"Yes"

"That's it," I said. "I will make an asparagus tofu stir fry."

"It's a deal," she concluded, and she smiled.

I told her that I loved her as she walked out the door. She smiled again.

My day commenced with a little Loreena McKennitt. She is Canadian, I believe. Her music sounds like a cross between Gregorian Chant and musak. I love it—so spiritually accessible. I took a shower in the Florence water that smelled like rotten eggs, with all that sulfur. My skin sparkled and I noticed that my hair was gray and shiny and thick as I drenched it in the shower, the first one I had had in weeks. My hair was what I had hated most about me—it stuck out in a crowd when I wanted to hide. It smelled funny after only a day. It frizzed out like a dandelion, instead of a rose. My mother pulled it and pulled it as she brushed it. Grandma said she did not know where in the family I could have possibly gotten it. Now that it was getting white, it was starting to look blond, blond with the sun's reflection. Not so bad, I thought.

My legs weren't as lumpy as I had remembered either. I had always thought that they sort of flared at the top into my big behind. Instead, this morning they looked rather relaxed and strong for an almost forty-year-old. And those teeth the size of Dentynes seemed natural, my smile special, which brought happiness to others. My belly, though still protruding, had a kind of majesty—made even more so by the plain fact that I had survived into adulthood, a matter of some debate when I was twenty and drinking and driving all at the same time down the middle of the George Washington Bridge at seventy miles an hour with a few drunken friends. I toweled myself dry, even my shoulders and the bottoms of my feet. Oh, look at my nails! Copper toenails. My feet had taken me a long way. Up mountains and Venetian bridges, in and out of people's beds, up and down the soccer field, to my dissertation defense. My feet had stood me straight up in front of my classes and pumped gas. They were always there, and I had never even noticed them until today. They were painted brand new and it was my job to take care of them. Who would if I didn't? It was my duty.

After my shower I put on those clean jeans, how luscious, and thought how lucky, I have a big talent. I can see ghosts—I bet none of my academic friends can. They may be better loved and better connected in their scholarly fields, but can they see ghosts? For the next conference on medieval music, I will suggest a panel dedicated to the exploration of professors who see ghosts and how they affect their scholarship. Mamma can't see ghosts. At least she never told me she could. I had to tell someone, so I called Valeria.

"Valeria, I am so glad that you are home," I said into my *nino*. "How are you feeling, my dear?"

"Not too well. I could not sleep last night. I had a nightmare about my sister. She had fallen down a flight of stairs." She paused. "What is it? You sound really excited."

"I can see spirits."

"Since when?"

"Miriam, you know, my friend the witch—she told me that I have a talent for it and that I need to nurture it."

"Really?" She seemed skeptically excited.

I hesitated. "Maybe I can help you?"

"How?"

"When you come to Venice next weekend, I'll show you."

"Can you see my sister?"

"Not yet."

"I hope that she is all right."

"I sense that she is upset." I paused and looked off into space. "Yes, she is very upset. Angry."

"What is she wearing?"

"I can't see that now. Come to Venice."

"Yes, yes. I will see you Friday afternoon. I think there is a train that will get me there at five-thirty."

"Good, I will meet you at the station. Love you," and I hung up.

I have to tell my cousin Chiara. I called her in Aosta and said that I hoped she didn't think what I was about to say was too strange, but that I could see spirits. Without hesitation she asked me how long I thought that my aunt, her mother, would remain depressed.

"Until your grandma dies." I began feeling stressed about telling people's futures.

"Makes sense," Chiara said, as if I had just told her how to avoid a traffic jam on the highway. Her mother was a bitter woman, refusing to go out of the house even for an afternoon.

So Chiara had to stay home and take care of her mother, who called her and every other female a *puttana* (whore). Being with my Uncle Mario was no picnic either. He was big and mean, and Chiara said that I should not worry, that she would not tell them my little secret because they were much too old-fashioned to understand. "Thanks," I said. "Speak to you soon."

I gathered my *nino* and diary and pens and guidebook and left the apartment. Making a right, I walked past the Palazzo Pitti; it must have been sixty-five degrees out this October day, and I was wearing too many clothes, which I peeled off progressively. I marched over to the Ponte Vecchio, crammed with ice-cream-eating folk with cameras dangling from their necks. Weary mothers with freshly graduated daughters looked inside pricey shops. Gold rings were lined up on red velvet trays.

I stopped at the first bookstore I could find to buy Miriam a present. I figured that with her witchy powers, which she used to write art history articles about Piero della Francesca, she could uncover the key to the succession of stories in the *Decameron* by Boccaccio. If she did that, she would be immortalized forever. The *Decameron* consists of one hundred stories, told by ten people on ten days. For six hundred years, no smarty pants from Harvard or Oxford has been able to unlock the secret to the sequence of Boccaccio's stories. Miriam could if she just put her mind to it. Then she could write an article about her discovery and be famous. This gift sounds perfect, I thought—it would challenge her powers to solve a literary puzzle. A strange young man asked me what I wanted and said that he had the Einaudi Edition I was looking for in the computer, and to hang on a minute while he found it in the store. His mother was behind the counter, behind the usual pile of books found in Italian bookstores, telling him that he was a good for nothing because it was taking him too long. "You don't even know where to look for that! After all these years. I am sorry *signorina*. You have to be patient with my son the fool. Really. Giorgio. And those pants? Why do you insist on wearing them to work?" She could see them while he was up on the ladder. "Please throw those out. They are not for you. They make you look like a slob." What this poor boy needed was the Liberty Bell. He could not find the book for me and said he was sorry. I said that I was sorry too.

Soon I came upon another bookstore in the Piazza della Repubblica. It was more American, corporate. Books were on shelves, and each shelf was marked with a tidy heading. A pleasant person stood behind a computer at the information desk and found the book for me immediately. They wrapped it in nice paper at the desk, as they often do in Italy even though it's no one's birthday. Next stop was the Internet café to email Barb and make sure everything was OK. Internet cafés are all over Florence, so I found one tucked away in a small room, empty, with a handsome guy smoking outside the door. He took my euros and gave me a card and said follow the directions on the screen, all in English.

As usual there was nothing of interest in my in-box. Just some forwarded mail from my college about the new Committee on Academic Performance. The president had announced that he put together the *crème de la crème* of the faculty to go over curriculum at the college and determine what stays and what goes. This was another paranoid maneuver from a typically paranoid bureaucrat: getting his buddies to overrule the will of the teachers. "Get rid of the history of women in music and teach Jefferson and the writing of the Declaration of Independence." Less music, more science! The more I thought of Mead, the sicker I got in my heart, and I made a pact that I would not think of or discuss the college during my sabbatical. They were scary and weird there, and anyway, what do academics really have to complain about? We have at least four months of vacation a year. Nothing can beat that.

The emails revealed there was no more love than usual—I think of email as a place where one should receive inspirational letters like "you're the best" from former students. I walked by the baptistery and the Duomo. Tourists sat on the pigeon-pooped steps and ate ice cream. The green and white and red marble façade of the church had been recently cleaned for the millennium celebrations, its black, sooty, bus-splattered patina wiped off with caustic chemicals, just to be replaced every day by some new dirt. Why Florence allowed cars and buses to rumble around its cherished *centro* was beyond my comprehension. It would be like letting cars drive through our national wilderness. Oh yeah, we do let that happen. Or like letting cars drive through wildlife preserves.

I walked into the Duomo—it was no charge—and looked up. It is bright and sparse, not like the churches in Venice. Huge arches cover flat pavements and Brunelleschi's dome hovers above it all, content to still be standing after all those years and wars. Miriam said that she had spoken in a trance to Brunelleschi a couple of weeks ago to ask him about some theatrical machinery he had designed. She wanted to know whether he had taught Donatello anything about the theater. Brunelleschi responded, "It is better than it sounds."

This sounded rather disjointed to me, but Miriam took it as a yes. Brunelleschi must have been a very ambitious person. His dome was so big. My dad's mother—my grandmother—was once rushed into the principal's office because her son had written the poem "I scratched my dome, for a poem" for an assignment comparing Shelley and Yeats. Sounded brilliant to me. Brunelleschi said, "I scratched my dome for a dome," and look what beauty he produced. Brunelleschi entered a contest to make the dome. Five people made wooden models—a woman among them. Her name is anonymous to this day. I walked around the edges of the church and remembered the time I had hauled my nineteen-year-old arse, with a broken foot in a cast from playing basketball, and on crutches, up the steps between the two domes Brunelleschi had designed, way to the top and out to see the view of Florence. Now you have to pay, so I didn't go up with my two working feet.

I exited the church stage left and drew in a strong cloud of diesel smoke, which I thought smelled really good when I was six. The museum was behind the dome to the east of the piazza. Tourists milled in front of it, and I was relieved that it was open today, because you never know in Italy. Sometimes it's Wednesday afternoon and a sign says closed. Or Monday mornings: *chiuso* (closed). They make it up as they go along. My luck was changing and I was floating around today. Sick to my stomach with joy. I bought some postcards of the marble Cantoria by Donatello, and wanted some slides, come to think of it. I needed one or two for my presentation in November in Toronto. The lady had what I needed and said to go over there— pointed—to get a ticket for the museum. "Grazie, grazie," I sang to her. But first I needed to go, and to my great delight the toilets were empty and clean. Still Italian style, though, which meant claustrophobic—I locked the door behind me in this narrow vestibule, like a vault housing family jewels. I did not sit on the seat, even though I did feel like tempting fate. Do you really get infections from toilet seats? What was I thinking! Of course—even though a woman's organ can fight off just about anything.

Finished, I washed my hands and dried them under the Italian dryer that was so strong it was about to singe the tips of my fingers. "Damn thing," I smiled, delirious.

I walked through some boring Roman ruins and a couple of busted columns when my cellphone went off. Shoot. I dug it out of my pocket to hear Paul's taciturn voice on the other end. "I've got some bad news. I won't be coming to visit you in Venice." I didn't respond, but felt sad. He was a good friend from my days as an undergraduate at Vassar. He went the banking route, even though he was a poet; I went the academic, even though I was a writer. Paul sounded unusually down.

"Jill left me."

"Why?" I asked, knowing full well. He had another full-time girlfriend named Debbie and had been juggling the two for five years—keeping them separate from one another with the help of a well-worn answering machine.

"I wasn't spending enough quality time with her."

Gee, I wondered, but remained compassionate and loving. "I am sorry." What did he expect was going to happen? Good thing one didn't find out about the other.

"I can't come because I have to stay here and get Jill back."

"What are you going to do?" I moved into a corner, near a marble relief of muscular horses.

"Tell her I want to marry her."

"Really? What about Debbie?"

"I will leave Debbie when Jill says yes."

"Have you been going to your shrink lately?"

"Yes, she says that I should call Jill and tell her that I am seeing a shrink and want to change and travel less."

Somehow I didn't think that Paul had told his shrink about Debbie and Jill. No matter. I felt bad for my old friend, who had watched me play basketball at Vassar and penned a couple of poems about it. He wanted to give me some gold earrings, which I told him to hang on to because I was gay.

"Gosh, I am sorry that I won't see you here. Venice is fantastic."

"I am sorry too."

"I'll call you soon to see how you're feeling. Love you."

"Love you too."

I walked up the stairs past Michelangelo's *Pietà* looking for Donatello. I wanted to talk about the musical angels in Donatello's *cantorie* (marble choir stall) and compare them to the angels in Padua. I walked into a huge, bright room filled with standing statues. Facing each other, on opposite walls about fifty feet apart, were the *cantorie*, one by Luca della Robbia and one by Donatello. They were outstanding white marble, rectangular structures, produced in 1438. I sat on a wooden bench and looked at the Della Robbia. Naked angels playing instruments looped around one another in marble relief. Below them, the museum had placed plaster copies of the musicians, and I noticed with some annoyance that people were touching them. And not only the copies—they were putting their hands all over the heads of the other standing statues by Donatello. I self-corrected and thought, people with the talent for seeing spirits shouldn't be critical and crabby about other human's' bad habits. We should rise above the mundane. But they were touching art! Shouldn't a guard put a stop to this?

As soon as I had stopped questioning myself, I noticed that the person who had had his back to me, touching the statue, had turned around. He was blind. A helper art historian was busy explaining the history of the Della Robbia *cantoria*, made for the Duomo at the same time as the Donatello. Then he guided his friend to a standing statue and told him that this was a Roman statesman and to touch the folds of tunic and feel how his feet stood on the ground in *contrapposto* with the weight not secure on one foot; to notice how Donatello has sculpted the hands crossing, in deference to his master, the Roman emperor. Tears began to form in my eyes. What a miraculous event I was witnessing. Art without sight. The appreciation of art in a completely tactile way. I love it when art works cross each other, like Laurie Anderson's line about architecture being frozen music, or musical pieces that were about pictures, like Mussorgsky's *Pictures at an Exhibition*. These people were doing art-crossing in their own heads. How profound and spiritual. I had sensed that great spiritual clues, about the meaning of life and love, lived in the cracks between the arts. If I could just find out the music made by the planets above, I would understand life. My feet were off the ground—I was rapturous. Rapture. What a concept. Depression. I was more used to its beige hues and plodding pressure. Rapture. Uproarious. I wanted to dance with the angels. Shouldn't I take a dance class? Maybe when I get home.

Soon I realized that the entire room was filled with blind folks and benevolent art historians. Amazing. Each blind person was touching the art, thinking, feeling. Learning more than anyone could at a stuffy conference. So profound. What could I say? And suddenly I thought it: Thank you, God, for showing me this. How strange? God? Oy, stop. Where has my cynicism gone? No matter. The people milled about and smiled. Two of them had their eyes closed shut. I looked up to see the Donatello Cantoria, its marble gleaming and figures dancing, and saw majesty. Donatello must have understood a greater power. My philosophy of life was changing before my eyes. My heart was so full of love that I thought it was going to burst and mess me up. Mom said to calm down, when I felt this way as a child. "You will die." Dante said to feel everything. "Don't be afraid." And you know what? I am still not dead. I am just not dying.

I gave the sculptures one last look, took some notes about the number of tambourine and violin players each had, and made my way downstairs. A wooden statue, about four feet tall, caught my attention and stopped me dead in my tracks. Donatello's Mary Magdalen. She looked at me with sorrow-filled eyes. Her long, dirty hair covered her torso, and her hands were clasped together in a gesture of prayer. She was still there. Still standing in her statue. Now was my chance.

"Mary," I said to her within. "You have suffered long enough. No need to hang around the statue anymore. Go and enjoy your afterlife. Go, I will support you." And I saw her spirit depart the statue and she smiled. "Holy moly!" I let out, shaking. Maybe Mary can help me with my worry-wart problem. I worry about everything—it's debilitating. We will see.

After purchasing a few more postcards in the bookstore, I made my way back toward the Palazzo Vecchio. Golden sunshine reflected off its medieval bricks. Back across the Ponte Vecchio I went in search of lunch, which today consisted of a veggie *panino* (sandwich) and a Coke at a self-service place. I read the *Herald Tribune* about the Yankees and Mets being in the World Series and didn't care for a second that I wouldn't be there to see the games. After wiping my mouth with the thin Italian napkin, I ventured back out into the warm sunshine toward Pitti Palace.

Never had I set foot inside the monstrous Pitti Palace or the fabled Boboli Gardens behind it. Dad said it was all too Baroque for him. But I had a new reason to visit: ghosts. What better place to hang out than in an old palace with manicured gardens? Another chance. I purchased a ticket and walked up a series of wide marble steps to the beginning of the exhibit of the permanent collection. The Raphaels caught my attention the most. A round Madonna and Child with a little bird occupied one of the palace's dark rooms. Raphael died very young, and one wonders what he would have accomplished if he had lived to the age Michelangelo did. One also wonders about Mozart, Schubert, Janis Joplin—though she probably would have burned out. It never occurred to me until just now to ask Raphael what he was up to and who he was living as.

I looked up at colorful ceilings filled with portraits of people looking down at me. They had small waists and little heads. Big dark bedrooms followed, the abodes of fashionable Medici descendents—no kings and queens like they have in France. Exhausted by all the images, I decided to take the plunge. Call Barb. I found a quiet spot on a marble banister at the entrance of the gardens and phoned her at work.

"Jean?"

"Yes."

"Hey, honey," she said warmly.

"Is this a good time to talk?"

"Yeah. I have a client coming in an hour."

"Dante and Miriam said that I have a special talent."

"You have many talents, Jean," she said kindly.

"I can see things."

"Well, what did you expect?"

"Yes,"

"Congratulations."

I was relieved. I had completely misjudged her reaction. She understood and loved me no matter what. What a gift.

"They told me that I need to open up more. See more. Feel things more deeply."

"Sounds good."

"Help people."

"With what?"

"Communicating with spirits."

I told her about how, in turn, the ghosts could help me achieve my life's dreams and overcome my depression. The depression that followed me around like a needy dog.

"I am so happy for you, Jean." She sounded sincere.

"Thank you, but Barb, please don't tell your parents or sister about this. They will make fun of me and think that I am stranger than they already do."

"Don't worry. It's none of their business."

Our conversation turned to our dog and her bowel movements and Barb's bowel movements, which were more regular than usual.

"I am glad that you are drinking less coffee," I said to her.

She said that her cases were keeping her really busy, especially the one about the high school drama teacher who was caught sniffing a line of cocaine on the floor of the theater.

"Poor guy," I said.

"He is in deep trouble."

We finished the conversation with our usual "love you"s, and I hung up feeling that I had made a great choice in Barb. This was often difficult to acknowledge because I had trouble commending myself for anything, including my choice of shoes today, which were gray sneakers.

I walked up the steep hill to look for ghosts. Miriam said to stare into space as if looking behind the object to see things. I did, but saw nothing out of the ordinary, just some gorgeous children throwing stones in a fountain. Children and dogs are godly, I thought. They feel things that are way beyond comprehension.

I arrived at a smaller, walled-in garden overlooking the countryside. It was as if I had come upon both sides of the coin. One side was a portrait, the other a pastoral landscape.

Behind the Boboli gardens stood villas on hillsides surrounded by pointy cypresses and rolling farms. Olive trees completed the vista. I stood in front of this landscape and looked into the distance. Looked next to trees and behind branches where ghosts usually hung out. Looked on paths and near a stream. Nothing, just a gentle warm breeze. Lovers stood near me, looking out. Others were eating their lunch. A woman in her thirties stood alone, an Italian for sure, with dyed brown long hair and tight jeans and a notebook. She stared out into the distance. I may have not found any ghosts, but I did find someone else who was looking for them. I could tell by her stolid gaze. Fear of rejection stopped me from talking to her. And a general feeling that I did not want to disturb her observations.

I skipped back down the hill and out the door of the Boboli gardens. The rest of the afternoon was reserved for writing and printing a first draft of my paper.

Chapter 8

The next day at Miriam's progressed in much the same way. I spent the morning looking for ghosts and the afternoon writing, until I had accomplished both my tasks: feeling ecstatic, and my paper. Miriam asked me whether I wanted a ride to the station and I said no, that I would rather walk. I had started a new regimen of walking as much as possible and eating sensibly—no problem in Italy. It is hard to find food that is really bad for you in this country. They just don't use preservatives or genetically modified foods and use only a few chemicals. It's genuine.

My train ride back north was smooth. When I arrived in Ferrara, I telephoned Lisa to see if she could meet me at the station. Stumbling to pick up the phone—it had dropped on the floor—Lisa answered and said that she was working that day but could meet me later.

"Let's meet in front of the Café Pedrocchi in Padua at six."

"Sounds perfect. I'll be at the library until then." I was thrilled. By the time I had finished ruminating about how my career was going nowhere at my college and missing Barb (bad habits are hard to outgrow, even with ghosts in the picture), I had arrived in Padua. I got off the train and began looking for signs for the "Santo," or church of Saint Antonio da Padua. The library was right next to it.

Padua is full of young people rushing off to schools—elementary, high school and college. Handsome people with colorful backpacks talking on their cellphones flooded the streets. I walked across a bridge and into the old part of town.

I remembered that the Santo was at the southern limit of the "centro" and oriented myself in that direction. Careful not to step in dog crap that lined the street, I notice two loud young women coming my way. They weren't dressed in the usual Italian woman's outfit. They wore dirty, baggy jeans and their hair was slightly disheveled. Happy to see them, I looked up and smiled gently. Just as they passed, one screamed something into my ear at full volume and then continued, laughing. My ear hurt and I lost it. Tears flooded my cheeks as I wondered what it was about myself that would have produced that reaction. Was I loathsome to look at? My reading of *The Art of Happiness* had made me understand that I am responsible for other people's reactions. I did not ask for this violence! When you are alone, things get magnified to an enormous degree, and not having Barb to talk to and process was the best thing for me at the moment. I thanked my lucky stars and felt better.

The library was down a narrow block, past the sprawling Prato della Valle, the largest piazza within city limits in Italy. It was oval in shape and contained all those male statues I had seen at Antonio's. The open air markets were here, today featuring antiques and other furniture. I walked by a stand that had souvenirs of Italy's Nazi past. How sickening. There were paratrooper helmets and swastikas. Old jackets and shoes. Another vendor had silver spoons and earrings. I looked at a couple of items and then regained my focus and went to the library.

A handsome man stood outside the library's main entrance. He looked at me carefully and followed me. He said that I needed to put my bag in a locker and fill out this green sheet with my name and address. I did and he told me to go up two flights of stairs. The marble stairs were gorgeous, and led to offices with large brown doors on either side. I walked in and gave my sheet to the librarian, who gave me a number and said the catalogue was in the other room. I was in heaven. Huge windows let warm light onto the desks. I looked up some things and gave the entries to the librarian. She showed me where the bathroom was after I asked. I walked up two stairs and locked the door behind me. Shit. It was one of those hole-in-the-floor toilets. No sitting platform. Meant for men. One had to turn around as if riding a motorcycle backwards, pee into a hole without splattering too much, so it wouldn't get on one's shoes, then get up from the squatting position to reach for a piece of toilet paper and thereby have the remaining pee crawl down one's leg anyway. But I was ready for this and grabbed a bunch of paper before I began to pee. Bastards. I outsmarted you.

I washed my hands in the clean sink and dried them under the requisite Italian blow dryer. Shit, I left my cellphone on. I reached into my pocket and turned it off. How embarrassing would that be for an American's cellphone to go off in the library. The little lady brought me the book I had requested, and I began to pour over its contents—a history of Lisa Cornaro Piscopia's life.

I was leafing through the book, looking to see if I could find the word "music," when I heard my name called out. "Professoressa D'Entreves?" "Yes." I looked up. The little lady walked over to me and showed me that I was not to run my finger over the manuscript while reading. "You could damage it with your skin oils." Forever ashamed of my manners, I asked for forgiveness, concerned that they would never allow me to handle the sacred books again, which were oozing of spirits.

Lisa Piscopia had Latin and Greek lessons as a child, when women weren't even allowed to look out the window without a chaperone. She learned how to sew and dance, too, and that's when a crazy music teacher entered her life. Magda taught her to sing and play the piano. They were inseparable for the next thirty years, for Lisa never wanted to marry, and had the money never to have to seek a suitor. A warm breeze blew into the reading room, shuffling the long, thick curtain. I wondered if I could see her. Dante's words rattled around in my mind again. He said don't ask why, just listen, feel, dream. Don't try to make sense of it—sense it. I ordered more books from the little lady at the desk, which were placed on a dumbwaiter downstairs. She yanked on the pullies to retrieve them. "Professoressa D'Entreves," she said in a sweet voice. "There is another book for you."

I walked over to her in absolute joy. What luck, what privilege I enjoyed to study the history of women. I read another brief biography about Piscopia and took some notes, copied a paragraph describing her music lessons, and returned the books with a smile. I smiled at the young women, who seemed college age, studying in the library. In fact there were more women than men here. They looked smart, and different from most of the women I had seen on Paduan streets, who were more interested in their skinny looks and made-up faces than in dusty books. There was something magical about people who liked to study. I glanced down at my watch and noticed that I had about forty-five minutes before I needed to meet Lisa at the café. It would take me half an hour to get there and I allotted fifteen minutes for getting lost, so I figured it was time to go. I'd study more another day.

I gathered my belongings in the locker downstairs and said "Good evening" to the man sitting behind the desk. He said, "*Buona sera, dottoressa.*" Wow, he called me doctor! And the feminine version too.

The streets in Italy are packed at five in the afternoon. Not with cars, as they are in America, with infamous rush-hour traffic, but with pedestrians and young kids promenading. They were showing off their finest clothes, slurping *gelati*. I did not see many Americans in Padua. The streets were as loud as an orchestra playing Mahler. Shops were full of people. The tables at the outdoor cafés were crammed with people drinking cappuccini and eating colorful deserts with flat cookies on top of them. I walked into a music store, searching for some sheet music of my favorite Italian seventies pop tunes.

I grew up on Claudio Baglioni, Riccardo Cocciante and Romina Power. Their songs were syrupy and kept me alive during my difficult and lonely teen years. I would tape them, put the beat-up tape recorder in my bike basket, and listen while I rode back from school. "Piccolo grande amore" was my favorite. It spoke of a man who falls in love with a woman because she is wearing a tight T-shirt, then dumps her because her love for him is too inconsequential. I loved falling in love with people because they were sexy. What else is there? Love meant losing oneself in another person's beautiful body. Italians singers sing as if they are going to die of unrequited love. Or lament that love is taken for granted. Young people killed themselves over love in Italy. That was a strange mystique that I felt too. Who knows how right I was? I only knew that I wanted to end my life for years because Gina Bacciagaluppi was not in love with me (she was sixteen), and had the most beautiful eyes. Then there was "Margherita," by Riccardo Cocciante. The words spoke of a love that would make him go into the sky and gather stars for her. He would write "I love you" all over the walls because *Margherita ama*, Margherita loves, and *Margherita è bella*, Margherita is beautiful. Beautiful. There it was again. So intense. It's only an illusion—we all have gruesome skulls and bones underneath. When I hear the song "Margherita," I am transported back to those high school crushes, their debilitating grandeur. Now, I just desired the sheet music.

With the sheet music, I could play all my favorites in the best way possible. "My way," as my composer friend used to tell me. He played Debussy better than anyone else because he played him the way he liked it. With the sheet music, I could repeat the same line over and over again, speeding up and slowing down when it moved me. I could dwell on particular chord changes and be ravished by the tears they could produce. The tears of remembrance. No one else was in the seventies sheet music section, and for this I was very grateful. Going through the endless selections required elbow room, pulling out their glossy covers, smiling and putting them back. I finally found a greatest hits compilation what was just that—all my tear-jerking favorites. I paid and tried not to look embarrassed to the cashier. It was like buying Neil Sedaka or Neil Diamond with tears flowing down your face.

Back in the Paduan air, my knapsack filled with clean clothes, my diary and a songbook, I sat on a stoop in the Piazza Pedrocchi and waited. A blond family of four, mother, father and two young sons, were singing original music. They were dirty and talented and the woman sang as the father tried to get the youngest boy to bang on a little drum. Italians put streams of money into their hat to help the family. The music was good, covers of Joni Mitchell and Paul Simon, and I wondered whether this was all legal in our day and age. How would the kids turn out? Would they be geniuses? The police did not ask them to leave, and a horde of people circled them, throwing off an aura of compassion. I pulled out a blank piece of paper and thought that I would draw a few things that I saw around me. It wasn't hard to find something fascinating. A lamp post, the arches of the school building.

Then I heard a song that had become familiar to me by now. It goes something like this: "Doctor, Doctor, Doctor of my Ass, Go to hell, go to hell, go to hell." It was sung by groups of friends of students who had just completed college and received their *dottore* designation (a rough equivalent to our master's degree). Clumps of young people followed one student, chanting, while the student listened, dressed in an outrageous costume. The woman looked like a whore, in high black platform heels and fishnets. She may be able to use her head in school, but she would need more in the real business world. Another young woman wore three-inch heals and a low-cut black cashmere sweater, her hair covering her shoulders. She was grinning as her friend feted her with "Go to hell, go to hell, go to hell." A polyphony, a kind of "Row, row, row your boat," ensued when another group of students sang to their favorite graduate. Charles Ives, in his own mind the father of American music, wrote symphonies that sounded like the collision of two or three marching bands. He would have loved this cacophony. On the walls of the university, artists hired by students had drawn caricatures of their friends with enormous genitals under skimpy clothing. After my dad got his Ph.D., the family history goes that Mamma said, "You are just as stupid as before you got your degree." Her philosophy could be traced to the drawings on the University of Padua walls. School in Italy was free, and so was the abuse. My mother had called me today, I forgot to mention, with incredibly good news. "What?" I asked, forever impatient with her.

"They installed a bidet in my apartment. Do you know how long I had to wait for it?" She sounded as if she had just won the lottery.

God had blessed me with colorful parents, I admitted to myself. I watched as a group of little Korean children ran in front of me to play on a contemporary art statue. They moved its heavy, bronze wheel and slid down its side. Watchful parents were close at hand. The kids spoke to each other in Italian. The world was changing. I would have never seen this twenty years ago. I checked my watch and noted that Lisa would be here in a couple of minutes. I drew a Roman column that was part of the building. Then I drew a marble window I saw to my left. The material to draw was unending.

I heard Lisa's high-pitched voice. She was dressed to the nines, because she was in fashion. She had on a purple wool skirt and top, purple alligator cowboy boots with two-inch heels and a matching beret. We spoke only in Italian.

"Am I late?"

"No. Perfect."

"Do you have any interest in seeing an art exhibit?"

"Sure."

She looked at my bag and decided that it belonged in her car immediately. "You don't want to carry that around with you, do you?"

"It's not so bad. I've been doing it all day."

"No, no. My car is parked under the supermarket over there. Let's get rid of it."

Her new blue, Alfa Romeo station wagon was squeezed into an Italian-sized parking spot and she opened the back door just a bit so I could wedge my stuff in it. "Fine, let's go."

We walked to the art museum across the street from the tomb of Antenor, the Greek founder of Padua. From my studies, I know that his remains were first found in 1274 and placed in that tomb and that only recently some unimaginative academic had them exhumed and found out that they weren't really his. Ruined everything. Lisa walked into the museum and asked for two tickets to see the show on Bolognese painting, and the lady said it was closing in ten minutes. "Oh," she whined. "It's too late. No matter, let's go shopping. I need to buy some shoes."

We walked toward the Santa Giustina Church in a pedestrian mall that was constantly interrupted by cars. Cars dropping off people and picking up stuff. A biker nearly hit us as Lisa was telling me about the president of an Italian leather company who wanted to go out with her. Being with Lisa was definitely weird because we were shopping and doing things I usually did with my mother. Being gay is confusing sometimes, especially around mother issues. The other problems, especially with me, had to do with pleasing. I am, after all, a woman, and there is enormous pressure in our culture to get approval from our fathers. I felt Dad's shadow over me intensely. Getting published, being with the dean of my little college, going to dinner parties with academics—all produced nausea in my stomach. They were the correct things to do in my profession and in my family, but they seemed all wrong in my soul. Whenever I went to a dinner party or other faculty event I felt nervous, as if I were with my parents. How weird.

Lisa marched me to her favorite inexpensive store and said hello to the sales women, as if they were friends. They treated us like Chinese Americans at a Chinese restaurant, with much more care and respect. I needed some shoes because I wanted to try to look a little more Italian. The femmiest shoes I can possibly wear are loafers, and that is because they aren't boots or sneakers. Lisa pulled out a couple of pairs for me to look at as she tried on some more purple shoes. Her stylish boots were hurting her feet, and she needed something else for the evening before her arches collapsed. I didn't really like the pair she chose for me, and looked around some more, until I came across some black, squared-toed, rubber-soled leather shoes. They looked masculine enough and wouldn't put the kibosh on my left big toe, the one that was treated by Silvana in Tuscany:

she had scraped the nail down to get off the fungus and now it was cracking.

Lisa asked me what I thought of the purple leather and loafers with heals. "Beautiful," I said quickly, in absolute heaven. "What do you think of these?"

"Nice," she said. "Very stylish."

We bought the shoes and walked over to her car. It was filled with cigarette ashes. Lisa peeled out of the lot at a blistering speed. "I see you wear your seatbelt," she said to me.

"Yes," I said, sort of embarrassed. In Italy, seatbelts were an uncomfortable nerdy accessory.

"I will put mine on too," she said triumphantly. "Every time I put it on I will think of my friend Jean."

That made me feel really good. She would think of me and stood a far better chance of surviving a car wreck.

We got out of Padua and drove toward the town of Abano. Lisa asked me if I wouldn't mind, after dinner, going to a party. Her new friend Paola, a "crazy woman," had invited us to a big party at some Persian people's home.

"Sounds good to me." As everything did in Italy.

"Great." She made a sharp right. "Let's stop here and get some pastries." We got out of the car and walked into the *pasticceria*. A woman wearing a wedding band, and the look of someone married for a long time, welcomed us.

"What can I get you?"

Lisa proceeded to ask for one of everything. Miniature eclairs, donuts, chocolate-frosted cookies, little custard-filled dough balls. The woman arranged them on a lovely platter and wrapped it with paper that had the name of the bakery on it, and then tied a ribbon around it. It looked like a birthday present, even though Lisa didn't think that the party was for anyone's birthday. She said her "crazy" friend was inviting her to lots of these strange parties. Last night they went to the theater, and later, with their thespian friends, over to her house. One woman, she told me, who was at least sixty, was wearing a red-leather miniskirt and had with her a twenty-year-old boyfriend. I laughed and laughed. How strange. Really.

We drove to Lisa's modest apartment building on the outskirts of Padua, which she said I could stay in whenever I wanted to. But I wouldn't want to because it was too far removed from the city. We walked up cold marble stairs to a third floor flat and she opened the door. It looked like a home no one lived in. Tidy and antiseptic. She asked me to leave my stuff in the first bedroom on the right and wondered if I might like to wash up in the bathroom next to it. I did and turned on the lights to a huge bright mirror where I could see all my pimples with ease. After getting a couple on my nose, I stopped myself from going whole hog and wrecking my face for the evening. It was tough, though. I knew that there must have been some real good ones, what with all this time of leaving my face alone.

She opened a bottle of prosecco for us to drink. It seeped quickly into my veins and felt great. She said that dinner would be modest, because who has time to cook anymore these days. "Next time, I'll make you my famous roasted vegetables. You will love them."

She boiled some ravioli in a pot and made some sauce out of gorgonzola and rosemary and garlic. What's not to like? She could have thawed a frozen dinner, then I would have been disappointed. She cut up some bread and made a quick salad with carrots and lettuce and radicchio. It was gourmet.

"I hope this is all right with you. I will do better in the future."

"Please, Lisa. You don't understand that this is fabulous. I usually eat tuna fish right out of the can with a little mayonnaise. Thank you so much for having me over."

"You are welcome, my dear."

She began to talk about her dysfunctional family, which is not called that in Italy. She has a twin sister, who doesn't look anything like her, and a violent brother, who still lives at home. He beats her eighty-year-old mother on occasion, when she doesn't get out of her seat fast enough. He has no money, demanding something monthly from Lisa, who gives it out of pity. "I tried to reconcile with him, Jean. I went to the psychologist for that sole purpose. But I learned that there is no such thing as a 'truce for one.' I don't want to see him anymore, and I go home only when he is not there."

Her brother's situation sounded a lot like mine, except for the beating part. My brother is a blossoming photographer, I told her. Handsome. He is a year younger than me and during his teen years smoked pot and got pissed off a lot. He harbored great resentment for me because my mother favored me growing up. I don't think she really liked him that much—isn't that awful? But luckily he took it out on me and didn't beat her. He yelled at me a lot and threatened to kill me on various occasions, especially after I told him that he was acting like a child after he punched a guy while we were playing pick-up basketball. Instead of killing me, he bashed his hand through his guitar. He's still angry after all these years, jumping down my throat at the most unprovocative thing, like telling him that I thought Patrick Ewing was great when he played for the Knicks. "No, he sucked!" he'd yell, his face getting red. "What the hell do you know, in Pennsylvania?" He still lives in the Bronx.

Before going to therapy and seeing ghosts, I probably wasn't the world's nicest sister. I was trying my hardest to be a better, more compassionate person. Frank was busy doing everything possible to make it into the high-powered New York City art world. He had an agent now to promote his art and he knew everyone in the business. He still ogled "girls" when we were together. Just last Christmas, our family went out to eat and Frank and Dad spent the entire time staring at a young woman across the way. Finally, knowing that I did not want to provoke war, I put my handkerchief over my eyes so as not to have to look at them. No one said a word.

Lisa told me about the time her father beat her so severely that she ran away from home and stayed two years with her uncle. Her uncle took her to the hospital to get the wound treated on her back, which required ten stitches. He had pushed her against a glass table. Her mother, who spent most of the day praying with rosary beads in her hand, stood frozen and never did a thing. "She is not educated. She only speaks dialect."

I listened with compassion and pictured what her childhood might have looked like. I imagined her bedroom, where she cried by herself, and the diary she kept to list her sorrows. After two years with her uncle, she left the house and took a job with Benetton, the Italian clothing manufacturer. She began in the warehouse, packing and shipping sweaters. Within two years they had moved her to sales, and by the time she was thirty, she was managing two stores herself. She left Benetton and bought a couple of franchise stores with another clothing company. She was wealthy, single and free by forty, when two disasters hit her at once. First, she was diagnosed with a tumor in her uterus. Second, she lost all her money.

While on vacation in Sicily, she had received a phone call from her doctor asking her to return home immediately—they had to operate. They removed the cancerous mass and put her on radiation treatments. After a time, they said that it was all gone. While this was happening, a Sicilian man took her money. It was relatively painless for him. He asked to be a partner in her business, she trusted him, and he emptied the bank account and left. When she went to the police, she learned that he had bilked many other entrepreneurs of their nest eggs, but there was no way to get him. He had covered his tracks and made it all seem legal. Not really. Reality was, she said, that no one messed with him because you could get yourself killed. He was part of the mob, and was protected on all sides by friends and family. She even saw him on the street once in a while. He wore shiny shoes and a freshly pressed suit.

"Jean," she confided in me, "I don't think that he has much longer to live."

"Why?"

"Someone he stole from is going to get real mad, and kill him. I guarantee."

This sounded way above anything I could handle. Too violent, too sick. Mafia people fascinated me—from afar. In a movie or on TV. They had no soul, no fears, no guilt. I stumbled into a Mafia family when I was in college. I dated a woman whose dad was in the mob. It was common knowledge. He was in the garment district mob. He was handsome, with a deep tan from sitting on the roof of his building with a reflecting mirror. He used to slap me on the back and say that he had a great investment for me, tampon dispensers. "You can't go wrong."

Lisa told me that she had picked up the pieces of her life in the last five years. She had borrowed a ton of money with which to purchase two beauty shops in Padua. One was in the mall, known as the Giotto Center. She was able to pay back her creditors, and then invested in clothing store in Adria, a town near the mouth of the Po. She said that she couldn't stand it when Antonio complained about how miserable his life was. "I have no self pity. I never cry. Just keep going. What other choice do I have? Antonio! Oh." She took a deep breath. "He acts like such a victim, as if he is the only one suffering. And does he try to do anything to make things better? No. He still calls his ex-girlfriend names, he still imagines that they will be together, he still says that it was all his wife's fault that his family fell apart. And there he is, in the villa all alone. There are women who would live with him there, be his companion. But he drives them all crazy with this whiney talk about how everyone is always out to get him. He should know better—he has flown all around the earth for Alitalia. Antonio. Antonio."

"Yeah. He can be a little over the top. But there is something about him that is so wonderful."

"Yes?"

"He lets you be yourself."

"And what is that supposed to mean?"

"He accepts a person's lot in life and does not try to change it."

She sort of shook her head. "He certainly is not a mean fellow. Just a pain in the ass."

She tidied up the dishes and brushed her teeth. Added a new coat of lipstick and fixed her hair and gave me the dessert to carry. She put on her high-heeled boots and checked her look in the mirror before escorting me out the door. Waving an address in her hand, she said that she knew exactly where this party was. In the country, near a shoe factory. Sounded fabulous, though it could have been in Flushing, Queens, and I would have been enraptured. I thought about talking to Lisa about my spirits. Somehow I knew that she saw them too and didn't want to be out-ghosted.

We looped around the outskirts of Padua, in and out of empty parking lots and driveways. "Damn it. Where the heck is this place?" Lisa said. I sat in blissful silence. She was not the type of angry driver that was disturbing, like my father, who slammed his hand on the car horn whenever someone did something to him. She was mad, but playful. Annoyed, yet jovial. "I promise you I will find the place," and she gave a quick call to her friend Paola, who said to follow the signs for Mandria and take the first left after the supermarket. "Yes, yes. Now I remember. See you soon." With confidence and a little impatience we sped into the distance and found an enclave of big homes. "This is it. I knew it all along."

Fifty cars were parked along the main road, and Lisa found a little spot at the end of them. Mercedes and BMWs were there, signs of nobility for any Italian family. Lisa spied her friend Paola walking with a man, and she honked so they would wait for us. Lisa made tidy introductions and said that I was American but spoke perfect Italian and understood everything. Paola was wearing black fishnets and a short skirt. Her brown hair was perfectly quaffed and she had family heirlooms on her neck. Her boyfriend, I assumed, had perfectly curly hair that fell to his shoulders, and bright brown eyes, even in the darkness. He held her hand firmly. Lisa said that they were thespians. I learned that word only last year, despite a Ph.D. and criticism from my family that my vocabulary was minimal. It's tough to be successful in academia without four-syllable words. I refuse to use the word prevaricate. Or preponderance. Not that I do not like words; I like to shape little words into big concepts, like notes into music. If I were a composer, I would use a lot of sixteenth notes, punctuated by rests. The truth is that compared to everyone else, I was hopelessly underdressed. It was making me get all self-critical inside.

We walked into the villa and were immediately greeted by the lady of the house, a dark beauty by the name of Alira. She took our coats and my Goretex jacket, which I had suddenly noticed was smelling a little stale from nervous overuse. She introduced us to her daughter Bettina, a sixteen-year-old student at the local high school.

"Jean is a professor of music," Lisa said with great pride. "In the United States."

"Really," said the lady of the house. "Bettina wants to go to college in the States."

We got into a brief conversation about that until I asked if I could have a glass of the prosecco on the table. "Sure," said the daughter. I chugged it down and waited eagerly for its effect. The kitchen was huge, remodeled in pine, with enormous counter space. How practical. The mother told us that she was thrilled that I could be here on such an important occasion. I nodded and asked politely, "And what would that be?"

"The Baha'i New Year."

"I see. I had no idea. I am sorry. I would have brought you a present." When in doubt, go into apology mode. It's sweet and sincere.

"No, no, my dear. Your gift is your presence," she said, equally genuinely.

What a concept, I thought to myself. "Thank you, then. Thank you very much."

It was strange speaking Italian with non-native Italians. Usually I speak English with non-natives. We all do in New York City. How wonderful that Italy was changing so that Italian became a second language. I walked into the spacious living room area to find Lisa and friends. To my great unhappiness, a big piano graced the room. Pianos in strange places often meant that I would be asked to play, and I always did badly because I don't know anything by heart and have a poor ear. No Suzuki method for me. I was trained in the Leschetizky method. All technique, arpeggios, curved hand position, exercises, and no horsing around. Result: big hand muscles, poor ear. Lisa was sitting next to Paola, who had her boyfriend on her arm. They made room for me in the middle, and Paola brushed her fishnet stockings up against my leg.

"Jean—" She paused. "Her eyes. I cannot stop looking into her eyes."

"Yes." I had no idea who she was talking about.

"Look how dark they are. May they never stop looking at me."

I finally realized that she was talking about Lisa, waxing weirdly poetic with dramatic exaggeration.

"She makes me so happy. Look at her smile. I cannot live without it."

Since she had a man attached to her, I really didn't know how to respond, and just smiled.

"Her skin is so soft." She looked down at the carpet. "All I want to do is touch her."

Oh, my. I wondered if she knew that she was talking to a closet lesbian. I tried to comfort Paola as she watched Lisa get up and go back into the kitchen, shaking her head. She had heard everything.

"What should I do?" she asked me rhetorically, and to her surprise I answered literally.

"Tell her that you want to go out with her."

She continued as if I had just said something completely inconsequential. "She makes my world—" more clichés. The problem is that I was getting completely aroused by the whole situation. By this time I was mildly inebriated. I needed to go to the bathroom.

"Sure, we will talk more. Look, Lisa is flirting with that man." She pointed toward the kitchen. Lisa was staring into a stranger's eyes. "She rips my heart apart. Damn her."

The drama was more than I could take and I got up to leave, when in the middle of the living room, the lady of the house clicked her glass and said that it was time to begin. "Begin what?" I asked in a low tone.

Everyone found a seat on a sofa or extra chairs; the kids found a little spot on the floor. I quickly sat down in a seat near the speaker and waited curiously to see what would happen next. The husband, Ali, was introduced next, and he very graciously welcomed his family and friends to his house. He then began with a little history of the Bahá'i faith, when it was founded and by whom. The fellow had an interesting name like "The Ba," which in Italian became translated to *Il Ba*. Ali told this and that story about the religion, which I quickly tuned out, as you can see, in favor of watching one of his sons seated next to him. As his father droned on and on, the little boy began making gestures indicating that his father was going on too long. He rolled his eyes and his hands. He stood on his head. He pulled on his dad's pant leg. He lay down on his dad's lap, until finally Ali thanked everyone for coming and wished us all a happy new year from him and his family.

I thought it was all very delightful and charming until the lady of the house announced that I, Jean, was going to grace this evening with a little piano playing. Nooooooo! I said inside. This cannot be happening. I gestured to her that I wasn't in shape to play a thing, but she insisted, using the words "bless this evening," over and over, until I felt that if I didn't, I would irrevocably harm the feelings of my hostess and embarrass myself in front of her friends. Who told her? It must have been Lisa. She wanted to hear me play. Drat. There was no way out. Problem is that I had no clue as to what to play. I had not a single piece in my fingers, and I have never improvised in public before. Not once. I had only begun to improvise in the last couple of years after one of my students taught me the blues scales and chord progressions. That was it. I would play the blues for the Italian Bahá'i New Year. Wish me luck. I saw no way out.

Thanking my gracious hostess and making a couple of excuses about not knowing anything from memory at the moment, I got up and did something I could have never imagined doing. Just playing. Just playing some notes. I did not have to please my mamma by playing the right notes: there weren't any. First, I placed my glass of prosecco on the piano, then picked it up again and took another gulp, pulled out the piano stool and sat down. After a quick warm-up of c minor scales and a quick test of the damper pedal, I began an idiotic, simple improvisation on the C blues scale. I remembered that people like it when you do flashy moves like fast runs, or parallel octaves and trills, so I threw them all into the musical stew. I played very quietly and then stormed to fortissimo and back to nothing—one hand alone, for greatest effect. People were listening intently, because I got completely lost in what I was doing, concentrating so hard not to just stop and fizzle. Keep going. Keep going. Inventing a melody, I put an ostinato harmony beneath it and thought about how lucky I was at this very moment. Alone, away from any critical voice. My mother would have been appalled and would have told me so. As would my piano teacher. Instead, when the music came to a stop involuntarily, as if guided by something bigger than me, everyone clapped loudly. And didn't stop. I got up and took a modest bow, and I heard someone ask me to continue, but no way. They kept on clapping and I thanked them for their attention. What had just happened? A miracle. Somewhere I had the found the courage to just play whatever came into my head in front of other people. It wasn't right or wrong, just me. What liberation from the dungeon of playing Bach, when I didn't have an aptitude for it. When every note was a struggle. I flew all over the piano keys tonight, thanks to my new friend Lisa.

After my tiny performance, people rose to congratulate me and Lisa snuggled up to me. "Jean," she said in her sing-song. "Did I tell you that the last three men I fell in love with are musicians?"

"No." I moved away from her.

"The last one was Marco. Oh, he played so beautifully." She grabbed my right hand. "You play exquisitely."

Backpedaling as fast as possible, I explained that I really was a good pianist, that I played at Carnegie Recital Hall when I was sixteen—OK so I bombed that day and every other day on stage in front of my mother and family, who said that my nerves were a sign of my deep selfishness. That if I only cared more about the music, I wouldn't lose myself and fall apart. Truth was my ear was so poorly developed that I memorized the music by rote, by touch, rather than sound. And when that memory was gone, I couldn't play. Maybe I could find my way around my room in the dark. Who needed that skill on stage?

Lisa led me back to her friends, while saying that Paola was strange. "She is very strange."

"She has a crush on you," I said proudly.

"She is very strange."

We interrupted a conversation about the new piano Paola wanted to buy for her living room. It had to be round to fit in just right, and circular pianos were expensive. In the meantime, she had maxed out her parents' credit cards to decorate the rest of the huge apartment they gave her from the family estate, which dates back to 1400. Paola was a Papafava, a member of one of Padua's oldest families. They had a cardinal in Rome once, Lisa informed me. "She is loaded."

Paola asked me what I was doing next weekend because she was having a big party at her house.

"Sorry," I said with much displeasure, "I have a friend

visiting."

"Bring her too."

"I don't know. She has suffered a terrible tragedy. Her sister committed suicide last month. I am not sure she is up for a party."

"Well, if you change your mind, give Lisa a call. You are coming aren't you dear?" Her tone changed to dreamy.

Clearly unnerved and seduced, Lisa replied, "What about your boyfriend? What are you saying?"

Then I realized that I was privy to something I had never known before: Italian debauchery. How exquisite. These people didn't need jobs, or have them. They went to parties and cultural events every night. They slept with members of both sexes out in the open. In America, we tend to hide our sexual proclivities in order not be ridiculed. Here they are a badge of honor. Paola was proud of the honesty and integrity of her crush on Lisa, and told strangers, even at Bahá'i New Year's parties. She was sensing the changes in her metabolism that accompany love, and she was ecstatic about them. Granted she did have a boyfriend on her arm. So what. He knew what was happening and still looked fondly at her. They were drunk or stoned. They were rich. He was an artist and designed sets for her theater. She kept him at her house, paid for everything and enjoyed the company of his exotic friends.

I could see, in my newfound psychological freedom, that I could be seduced quickly and get lost in this culture. We could start drinking at eleven, having sex at three, a nap, lunch, then a promenade to the piazza and chats with friends. Dinner out at a friend's house, more booze, (in my drunkeness, I would cut off connections to my old world, Barb and family friends) a video, and everyone would have sex together. The next day we would take her boat out on the Brenta River (near Padua) and sail toward Venice, stop at a villa and meet an old friend, who would invite us in for coffee. I would be on one arm, her boyfriend on the other. No questions asked. I would be introduced as a poet of little regard, an ex-pat who despised the frivolity of the American lifestyle. We would all have sex on the veranda and eat duck pate afterward and get a tour of the villa's fine oil painting collection. Then they would take us out on a drive in their Mercedes convertible, up toward the Dolomites, my hair flapping in the wind as it sprouted out from beneath my silk scarf. Paola would kiss me gently on the cheek and ask me to recite my newest poem. "Please, for me?"

I would hesitate just a bit, so that she would ask me again, and say some delightful quip about Flannery O'Connor's disdain for something or other. "Isn't she talented?" Paola would utter at the end, after my silly lines.

"You are a strange person." Lisa returned me to reality.

"Stop, my ripe plum. You are mistaking my shortness of breath around you for anxiety. It is something entirely different."

We drank more prosecco and thanked the lady of the house. She got our coats and led us to the door. Our magical evening was over and Lisa drove me back to her home, where I quickly fell asleep on her big matrimonial bed, while she slept in her own room.

The next day I was overtaken by feelings of joy, like on a sunny, hot spring day playing soccer. For the first time since I was ten years old, I thought that the endless possibilities of the world had been given to me by a higher spirit, instead of being restricted from me because I was a woman and an outsider. Grabbing my toothbrush and once again refraining from picking my zits, I felt free and lucky to be alive. Lisa said that she would drive me back to Venice, until she got a phone call from a guy named Guido, who said that he would be right over to take her for a drive into the country.

She prepared me a healthy breakfast of bananas and muesli and we took showers and listened to Bob Dylan's music. She asked me if he was my favorite and I said no, but close. I had no favorite, except for Stevie Nicks, who could do no wrong in my book, even after she left Fleetwood Mac. The doorbell rang and an extraordinarily elegant man walked in. He had gold rings on his fingers, which looked, if my eyes weren't mistaken, like American class rings. How strange. He said that he collects them along with cars. He owned the same kind of Lincoln Continental that Kennedy was shot in, two Bentleys, a Corvette—all in Italy. Debauchery. Lisa said that his father owned a marble quarry outside of Verona. Guido vaguely managed the family business, when he wasn't racing boats in the Adriatic. Was this Lisa's boyfriend? I wonder if he played the piano.

Anyway, they dropped me off at the train station in Padua and said the Italian equivalent of "So long, sucker. Sorry you have to go back to your studies." Somehow their level of play was far beyond what I was used to: a few beers after a soccer game, a kiss on the promenade, an occasional late night of disco dancing in the early eighties, an affair with a married man. But nothing could dampen my mood today, and I had much to look forward to, anyway. Valeria was coming to visit. Her train was getting in at five and everything had to be perfect for her. I needed to clean the house and buy some things, perhaps a little present for my dear friend in need. I once wrote a poem when I was thirteen that began, "I wish I could mend, the problem of my friend." So adolescent, yet so precise.

Chapter 9

Five o'clock rolls around a lot faster in Venice than it does in Pennsylvania. By the time I had done my errands, spoken to Barb on the phone, read a Xeroxed article, as part of my research, and bought Valeria a glass mother fishy with four little babies, it was time to walk to the station. Sometimes Italian trains get to the station early. I bounded over the Ponte degli Scalzi, up into heaven and back down, jumped the train station steps two at a time, and found Valeria's train on the *Arrivi* board, coming in from Bologna. It was coming on *binario* ten, and I rushed over at 4:56 to wait for her, along with tourists waiting to take the train back to Bologna and continue on to Florence.

Short men on electric carts honked at me, and I jumped out of their way. I avoided the bands of nervous smokers and pigeons that infiltrated the complicated semi-covered train station. A train came into the station on track ten, and I hoped that it was hers. A little distracted by a sudden daydream about my annoying and mean-spirited boss back at the college, I saw Valeria appear directly in front of me as if she had materialized. She called my name and I smiled. She looked terrible, like someone had died. Skinny and drawn, her face had lost its luster. Her hair, still blond, was clumped in thick strands. She wore light blue denim pants and a maroon sweater. A gray, beat-up plastic fanny-pack was strapped around her waist. She carried a dirty black knapsack over her shoulder. Her blue eyes punctured this distressing picture of my friend's suffering. And as much as she tried, her smiles could not blow away the cloud over her face when I hugged her, firmly.

We stood together like this for longer than usual, her head only reaching my shoulder. In Italy people suffer silently more than in America, I deduced, because it was un-Italian to complain about a bad thing that had occurred. In that sense they are more like the British. Complaining may be a naively American thing to do, but at least one might find comfort in a friend or stranger or shrink. My shrink in Pennsylvania had heard me complain for years. She thought it was good for me.

Valeria said that she had brought some fresh radicchio for dinner. "Do you have any pasta?"

"Tons."

I asked her if she needed help with her bag and she said no and we walked into the warm Venetian air. She smiled and her radiant person was released for the first time in weeks. I directed her to my little apartment, where I suggested that she leave her stuff and wash up if she liked. Then we could go for a nice long walk to the Piazza San Marco. She couldn't think of anything better and locked the bathroom door behind her. I picked up my little plastic recorder and blew the Riccardo Cocciante song that I loved, "Margherita." Valeria recognized it, despite the quality of my rendition, and began singing the lyrics, *Io non posso stare fermo con le mani nelle mani* (I can't stay still, with my hands in my hands), *Quante cose devo fare prima che venga domani* (I have to do so many things before tomorrow comes).

"Oh, Jean, I remember now how much you loved that song."

After crossing the Accademia Bridge and reaching the ample open space of the Piazza Santo Stefano, Valeria asked me if I'd been to see the Conservatory.

"It's around the corner."

We walked in the shadow of a narrow passage and came upon busts of musicians and an elegant atrium. We walked in and moved out of the way of beautiful young people carrying instruments. Valeria said that she once was on a panel here about women composers. She pointed me in the direction of a bulletin board and we looked at the program.

"Look," she said excitedly, "There's a festival about Luigi Nono, the avant-garde composer who died a few years ago." She checked her watch.

"They're showing a documentary movie about his career. Do you want to go?"

"Sure." How could a musicologist resist?

She grabbed my hand and led me up a flight of stairs. We tried to buy tickets from two skinny girls seated at the table, but they just said, "Don't worry about it," because the film had started a while ago. We walked through thick red velvet curtains into a jam-packed auditorium. No seats in sight, we found two spots where we could lean against the wall. Valeria smiled at me broadly, and I was so glad that I could participate in distracting her from the pain of her sister's suicide.

We watched interviews of Nono, an extraordinarily handsome, tall Venetian, who spoke to Franco Donatoni, Valeria's composition teacher.

Valeria elbowed me and said, "He wanted to sleep with me too. He was quite the Casanova."

The thought made me sad, and I recalled the stories I'd heard of young women composers forced or, better, coerced into sleeping with older men in order to be embraced by the musical establishment. After they slept with them, they became their secretaries, and in the case of Clara Schumann, edited all the husband's music. Stopped composing their own.

Valeria had followed a similar career path; she slept with Donatoni for six years and pumped up his ego. He brought her to music festivals and introduced her to important conductors. Though forty years her elder, she said they had great sex, fanciful and energetic. Then he died and she was left to fend for herself, which she did by landing a job at a small conservatory in Reggio Emilia. She taught theory and ear training to appreciative teenage students, and made the half-hour commute back to Modena, her home town, four days a week. Valeria never got her driver's license and walked around with a thick train schedule in her knapsack at all times. Cars were a luxury she couldn't afford.

After Donatoni, she found a boyfriend named Taddeo, a Venetian by birth, who taught computer science at the University of Padua. They were introduced at a party and she fell in love with his nerdiness and he with hers. He eventually bought a big apartment for them in historic downtown Modena, which they shared on weekends, he living in Padua during the week. At first things went smoothly. They attended faculty parties and mingled with each other's families. Valeria developed a strong bond with Taddeo's rich and opinionated aunt, and they confided to each other their infidelities and frustrations with men. Valeria, sensing that Taddeo had "girls" at the university, kept herself busy as well by being seduced by the porter at the main Modena train station and later an old professor she had met at her yoga place. Their lives were rich and miserable, neither confronted the other's affairs, and both continued despite their fears of losing each other—until the day Taddeo's aunt told Valeria that there was another woman in Taddeo's life, and this time it was serious.

"You must do something," she warned Valeria.

"What?"

"Meet someone else more appropriate for you."

Valeria could not confront him and continued to throw herself into affairs with married lovers. She completely stopped composing, could not even sit down at the piano. Putting her thoughts into music was not an option. She became completely clogged up with jealousy. Many times I wondered whether she might not fancy a roll in the sack. She had lesbian friends besides me, like the violinist in Florence and a gal at her yoga place, but she never slept with them. About six years ago, when I visited her to write an interview, I had a strong sensation, after a bottle of wine, that she wanted to sleep with me. She snuggled up to me and talked about Taddeo's other woman, and a part of me wanted to turn to her and kiss her and make her mine. But then I was reminded of the STDs, and she was sleeping with strangers, and how I had gotten one for the rest of my life. Though I was attracted to her, I declined smartly. Valeria was a Gemini, and I a Taurus—potential for heavy tragedy. She was undecided, I too decided, and ultimately I realized that if I fell in love, she wouldn't know what to do, and she'd leave my heart in shreds.

We watched the documentary for about fifteen minutes. The audience clapped politely and the lights came on. A large professor from the University Foscari introduced himself as a Nono scholar and pointed to Nono's aging and glamorous wife, thanking her for her assistance with the festival. She wore her hair like a bulb above her head.

Valeria said that she'd been cuckolded a thousand times. Some women found great strength in their resolution to stay with their man. It felt a little like circular reasoning to me. And while the large man boasted about the scores—Nono had made him his musical executor—we moved to the front of the hall to some empty seats.

"Why do women stay with these kinds of men?" I asked Valeria.

"Power."

"But they have none."

"Not true. They tell their husbands what to do and how."

"So what. They are degraded by their affairs."

"They learn to live with it. Better than being alone, or with some bore. Then they make some children, who they can show off."

"I see."

The big guy asked that the director of the film come to the stage to answer a few questions.

A tall, skinny but handsome filmmaker type walked modestly to the front, with all the confidence of a cherry tree in bloom. People clapped and asked questions. There was no mike, so no one heard anything. Valeria marveled at his egoism.

"Remarkable, at such a young age," she said.

We talked a little about Taddeo's new wife, Sandra. She was a former student and, like Taddeo, from a well-to-do family from Venice.

"They are better suited. Both cold, living too close to Austria," Valeria said. "He was so calculating, he even made provisions to buy me a little apartment in Modena when he left me. Never spoke to me about her. Just gave me the keys."

The German filmmaker replied inaudibly to questions and the event was over after a smattering of clapping.

"Good thing we only caught the end," Valeria said. I loved her dry sense of humor and laughed out loud.

We continued toward Piazza San Marco as the light dimmed. It was around seven and we were hungry. Valeria said that she wanted to get a snack before we went home to make dinner. We arrived in the Piazza San Marco from the west, to the sounds of bands playing Italian jazz and children chasing pigeons. The sky was a gray-blue in the warm night air, and we passed by the tall bell tower. Valeria pointed to a little café on the corner beneath the portico.

"That's fine," I said.

We walked into a bright, glassy room with few patrons. A handsome man behind the counter wearing a black-and-white uniform immediately asked us what we wanted. Valeria eyed the *tramezzini* (little finger sandwiches on white bread). They were filled with egg and tuna salad. "Yummy." Valeria grinned at my word. "I'd like one of each," she said.

"Me too, and let's get two glasses of prosecco."

"Yes."

The waiter placed our goodies on the counter. And that's when I saw her for the first time.

"Valeria." I touched my friend gently. "She is here. Your sister is standing over there."

I could make out her elbows leaning against the counter. She was wearing a light-blue cardigan sweater.

Valeria stepped away from the counter with her prosecco glass and looked.

"I don't see her," Valeria said softly, trying not to disturb her. Tears quickly filled her eyes and came down her cheeks.

"She is there and smiling and happy to be with us."

"We used to come to this café when we were teenagers, to get away from Modena for the day."

"You can speak to her if you like."

"What shall I say?"

"Tell her that you forgive her for what she has done and that you love her. She is very anxious and needy. Tell her that she does not need to suffer anymore." As I said these words, which seemed strange to my own lips, I watched Valeria mouth words to her sister. I was watching a miracle.

We stood in silence and finished our proseccos. I had a sickening feeling, as when I passed my Ph.D. exams, that perhaps I was full of it. What happens if what I was seeing wasn't true? That Angela was not there? That what I had communicated to Valeria was just not true? Then I remembered what Dante said. "Believe in what you see. What you see is what is true."

Valeria wanted to know more, and I could see how easily people in pain could be manipulated by people who see ghosts. I told her that her hair was tidy, and that it came to her shoulders. I said that her eyes looked as if she was still suffering. (In reality, I thought that Angela looked really angry, still blaming others for what she had done. She still wanted retribution and was back now to teach Valeria a lesson. *Don't forget* about the people you love. They can die at any time.)

Valeria said that she had just found out from Angela's son that Angela had told him his dad was cheating on her, and that she couldn't stand it. He told Valeria that she was really angry the night she died. He asked Valeria to tell him the truth they were hiding from him. Valeria said again that the car accident was the truth, and so the web of lies continues even after someone passes on. I did not enjoy meeting Angela's ghost, I thought to myself. She had as much make-up on as Tammy Faye Bakker. She looked tiny and mean, vindictive—must have been all the medication they put her on. Valeria said that she was over-medicated, being treated for depression, anxiety and weight loss.

Valeria talked about the time they went to Sicily together, but my mind wandered. Dante said that I could learn something from seeing ghosts. What? I struggled. What could I possibly learn in this instance? I learned that ghosts did not frighten me

I tried to communicate that to Angela through my thoughts. I felt that she needed to forgive herself for what she had done, but the reality was that Angela was far, very far from doing that. She was pissed. Pissed at Valeria, her son, her miserable husband. I do not do well with pissed off people. My dad was always pissed and he frightened me. She did a little too. Dante also said not to interpret what I see. Just see. Do not reason or judge. Learn to have faith in my senses, and let go, let go.

We finished our snacks and I felt intoxicated. Not by the prosecco, but by sharing the experience with Valeria. I had never talked about spirits before while watching one. It all seemed very personal, and a little neurotic. Talking about what I had seen made me seem saner to myself, and my path to becoming an artist was beginning to take shape in the distance. Imagination and the sublime and the divine were on a continuum. Dante said that Michelangelo and Leonardo could see spirits. He said that all the great spirits had seen spirits: they told only their best friends about them. Spirits infiltrated their art, and they had no chance to do anything else. Like a potato on your kitchen counter for two months, it has to grow sprouts.

Through Angela's spirit I began to understand my need to be creative, the urge that put me in such a precarious position—in professional and family life. Professionally—that is, in writing about fifteenth-century music, my dissertation, conference papers—I always had a sinking feeling that I was going to be found out. That people would see through my façade of being a serious scholar, the person who read all the literature, wrote all the nice footnotes. But instead of writing scholarship, I was writing history about music that was completely from my heart. I felt an urge to write my books—they were not modeled after any others I had read. I could not model. I could not model anything, because when I did I felt in my heart that it was not ME. It did not feel right. So my writing was always different. "Why can't you just be like other kids?" my mother would ask—and the dean, when they tried to deny me tenure. "Why can't you follow the rules?" Phooey. So I got depressed and self-hating and self-doubting and wished my life would end.

Spirits were the answer. They would help me. And this was just the beginning.

Valeria told me that she had spoken to Angela's shrink recently. The shrink was distraught and wanted to see Valeria in her office. She felt completely responsible for what had happened. She had seen her sister every day for the two weeks before the suicide. She had called her every night before she went to sleep. She had urged her sister to check into the hospital. She had begged her. Valeria said that she did not have the space to show the shrink compassion; she needed a shrink herself.

How bizarre! This time we took another route home, via the Rialto Bridge. The bridge is the oldest over the Grand Canal and cuts it in half, in the middle of the city. It is surrounded by Renaissance *palazzi* (palaces) soaking in the water. After crossing it we landed in the mecca for souvenir hunters. Men and women sold soccer jerseys and miniature gondolas and little leaning tower of Pisa's. Hey, it's Italy. Valeria said there was a market we could go look at over on the right. The old fish market, closed now of course, but that's where it is, on the platform near the Grand Canal. We stopped in a health food store to purchase cookies because Valeria did not eat processed sugars. We needed some bread for our meal. I assured her that I had plenty of pasta in the cupboards—who didn't in Italy? Pasta was like ketchup in America.

We walked in the dim and narrow streets, making room for ladies with their dogs, which took an occasional poop in the street, which the ladies covered up with a hanky. It's a trap, I thought. We zipped over to the Campo Santa Maria Mater Domini as Valeria spoke about her sister's experience in law school in Modena, and how she graduated at the top of her class. She had taken a job at a real estate firm, but then shifted to working for the city, wanting to be more of an activist for the common good. She had just gotten a job as a manager in the local government, overseeing schools. She was a popular big cheese, if there is such a thing. But recently Angela had felt the pressures of the job, getting little sleep and fearing that she might get passed over for a promotion by a prettier, smarter woman. Angela's husband, the vice-mayor, had said he would not let that happen. But he was having an affair with his secretary. Someone in her office had spotted them together, looking romantic at a local café. How silly they looked, in love, the woman told Angela. The dissent into madness began, and it lasted, Valeria told me, for six months. She was losing weight. Not sleeping.

"I brought the suicide note for you to read."

I had never seen a suicide note. Only heard about them in the movies.

"I also wrote down my feelings the other day. Could you read these, too?"

"I would want to do anything to comfort you, my dear friend."

The School of Saint John the Evangelist was on our right, and I knew that we were close to home. The school was having a concert that night of Vivaldi's *Four Seasons*, and we saw the orchestra players walking to the building with their instruments. They looked late and were wearing eighteenth-century costumes. We reached my apartment on Calle de la Laca and unlocked the door. I took Valeria to the bedroom that we would share for the night and said that she could lie down, that I would make dinner. But she wanted to make me dinner and that was that.

Valeria made spaghetti sauce out of radicchio, garlic, and onions. First she fried up the garlic and onion in olive oil and butter, until they were yellow. Then she threw in handfuls of chopped radicchio, and sauteed everything briefly. Then she dumped the penne pasta in the saucepan and added some Parmesan cheese, and it was ready to be served with a nice slice of bread and Italian mineral water. She ladled some on my plate and sat down. Out of the corner of my eye, I noticed that Valeria's sister was seated on a chair in the living room. I did not have the heart or the confidence to tell Valeria that she was there, so I just looked at her, and this time got a good clear impression of her.

She was skinny, with brown eyes and hair. She had dimples, even when she didn't smile, which she wasn't. Her face was wide and her eyebrows thick, her eyelashes heightened with make-up. She had on brown wool pants and a green sweater that covered a white cotton, button-down shirt. Her hands were placed by her side, and neither had a wedding ring. She looked directly at me, and asked me a question. "Why did he do this to me?"

I responded, "Forgive him. Forgive him and your family."

"I can not."

"You must. I will help you."

Valeria asked me a question.

"I am sorry, what did you say?"

"Do you like your pasta? You haven't said a word."

"Yes, my dear. I am so sorry. It is exquisite."

But Angela would not let it drop. "He ruined my life."

"He did not mean to, and if he did, you must forgive him even more."

"I hate him."

"You are stubborn, Angela."

"So are you."

"True. But we are talking about you right now."

"Who are you? Just because you can see me . . ."

"You have come to me for help, and I can help you."

"How?"

"Accept your fate. Accept yourself. Go and live happily in the next world."

"Easy for you to say."

"Not really, it's rather weird."

"I need to talk to Valeria."

"Go ahead."

"She can't hear me."

"Try. She might be able to hear you in a dream."

"Valeria, my dear sister. You have been a cold and brutal person to me. Leaving the family. Never even a phone call at Christmas. You abandoned me."

"Keep going."

"I missed you. Your advice, your smarts and your devotion to what is beautiful. And you too are making the same mistakes."

"Help her."

"Be careful of Cesare. He cheats on you daily."

"How do you know?"

"I saw him with another woman the day before I died."

Valeria got up out of her chair and reached for a bottle of wine. "Would you care for some?"

"Yes, yes, my dear." I heard the cork pop and Angela was gone.

"You were thinking of my sister, weren't you?" Valeria confronted me.

"Yes, she was just here, and now she is gone."

Valeria walked over to her knapsack and pulled out a well-worn envelope. "I want you to read this. It is the letter she left on the passenger seat of her car. It's her suicide note.

It was printed on her computer, with perfectly formatted margins and in New Times Roman font, 12 point. It was addressed to her husband, Luigi.

September 2, 2001

Luigi,

Your eyes do not light up for me anymore. You spend nights at the office and leave me to fend for myself with Roberto. You have found another woman and you discard me like an old pair of shoes. I despise you. Your smell sickens me. The sound of your breathing fills me with rage. When we met eight years ago, you changed my world. Night was day and day all the time. I lived and breathed for you, my handsome man. Your strength was a source of comfort. Strength I could never muster in any respect. I am a cowardly person, a disgusting and ugly individual, no one will miss me. I do not do this to harm Roberto. I ask you to take care of Roberto, find him a good nanny. Use all my money in the bank for him. Good night, Angela.

The note filled me with profound sadness. Her anger was obvious—she did the ultimate act. She had the ultimate revenge. She would make all suffer until they died. Suffer wondering what they had done to produce such unhappiness. She was the road-rage driver on a destination of destruction. Only it doesn't quite work that way—at least that is how I have been feeling recently. A person doesn't just disappear off the earth. Memories, smells, stories and lies keep them alive. Memories are divine. The imagination is sacred. And Angela has been here with us, again, still angry. Until she releases her rage, she will torment the living and those who have passed on.

Valeria pulled out some documents regarding her sister's death, which she had gotten at the coroner's office. Time of death, 2:32 a.m. Death by carbon monoxide. There was an account of the young man finding her body and pulling her out of the car. Valeria said that Luigi never went to see the body, but asked that Valeria identify it for him. She pulled out some of the medicines that had been prescribed for Angela. She pulled out a short obituary in the Modena newspaper, announcing the suicide. We looked at the material, like detectives on a case, trying to understand her motivation and ours for not being available to help a lost soul. Too caught up in our own battles.

Suicide has a way of pushing families and friends apart. One would expect the opposite. Instead, families retreat inside a cocoon of questions. Why? What could I have done differently? Valeria's parents did not attend the funeral. They said they were too sick, but Valeria said it was embarrassment. They will be judged by other families, snickered at by people who believe that this could never happen in their family. Valeria's little sister, who still lives at home, blames everyone else for abandoning Angela. She screams at the top of her lungs when she is alone, in despair.

Valeria's two brothers occupy the middle positions. The first, Fausto, is an artist and writer who lives by himself in Turin, trying to scratch out a living. He wrote a book about the stupid things people say when they are at the airport, and drew pictures. He composes songs and had a CD or two of his songs put out by a very small label. Sometimes he lives in the train station for a month, when he has no money left for rent. Then, when he gets a gig, he goes back to living in the small hotel and can pay his way again. Tommaso is a banker in Modena, married with two children, the most traditional of the bunch. He came to the funeral with his family and hugged Valeria when it was all over. He met her after for coffee and they exchanged photographs of Angela. No one else in the family would look at them. Suicide happens in many families, he reminded Valeria. It had happened just recently to a big industrial family. Someone in the Fiat family had jumped off a bridge. Valeria and Tommaso shared their stories of childhood and went over to their parents' home only briefly, to buy them some groceries. Their parents did not speak about Angela. Five children in an Italian family is quite rare, and instead of coming together, they fled away into their thoughts.

Valeria gave me a brief poem she had written about her sister. It read like something by Yeats, except in Italian. Lyrical, with great vocabulary, it was enchanting. Then she said that she was working on rap lyrics, for which her brother Fausto said he would provide the music. He wanted to produce a CD dedicated to their sister called *"Vola, Angela"* (Fly, Angela), and the rap piece would fit just fine. Valeria was invited to go to the studio next week to begin recording sessions. They will use the money to pay for the upkeep of her sister's grave in Modena. Grave management is an art in Italy, where tombs have elaborate floral designs and photographs to keep clean. At least Fausto would talk to her, in sensitive, grandiose language about how much they miss her and how responsible they feel for her death, being so immersed in their own lives.

Valeria said that she had had a nice visit from some of her sister's law school friends, who had come by to share memories last week. They brought some old pictures of Angela in her early twenties, smiling and working hard. She had her first serious boyfriend in law school, and they noticed that she was obsessed by him. Valeria said that she was obsessed about a lot of things, including her weight and her hair, the color of which she kept changing. The women were so friendly. All felt guilty—all agreed that they could have done more for Angela, and would do more for each other given that they are still around. They had kids, many happy little children. Their backlash is against having children and marrying men they will have to care for. Their mothers had given them unpaid servants as models, not humans, cleaning underwear, preparing food, washing the house, and while they were cuckolded.

Italian women were fiercely independent, and the thought of the old ways sent them running away from marriage and children. Especially children. Italy's population is in continual decline, and that was just fine with them. My mother worked for me all my life: made every bed I ever slept in, did my laundry in college (she would come visit me and pick it up and drop off clean laundry), and fed me. It wasn't until I was thirty-five that I learned how to separate the lights from the darks. All my white sport socks are still some shade of pink or purple. And look at me: no kids, no husband. Same for my brother. Except that my brother is looking for an Italian woman to be his wife-mother. How hard is that in New York City?

My experience with my Italian family was very different from the one with my American family. My Italian family spent a lot of time together, acting as if they couldn't stand one another. So did my American family, but we saw each other less, so it wasn't as painful. My Italian family doesn't say how they feel. My American family is verbal and opinionated and cold, too. They believe that family, traditional marriage, is a bore, and my dad thinks that sex outside the marriage is perfectly noble and necessary to survive. Only stupid people got married. How boring and wasteful. My American family derived its sense of exaltation, the way you feel when you are in love, only from unrequited love. Exultation in nature or God or the sublime was not an option. So, when I was young, I kept looking for lousy love affairs to get that high, that transcendence. Bad idea. My dad did it too. But he could do it, because he always had his wife-mother to return to. Like moss on the roof, she would never leave.

Believing that exaltation can only come from sex causes many problems. Sex outside the marriage can cause deep scars, no matter how glamorous some fathers try to make it seem. I got depressed because I continually needed a fix, so when I was in a good, stable relationship, I dumped it—no exaltation. The trees provided me little solace, the sea only anxiety, the mountains a sense of urgency that I needed to go down. Flowers meant funerals.

My cellphone rang, and I excused myself politely and hoped that it was Barb. Instead, it was Antonio. Antonio wanted to know whether I might like to come visit his villa next weekend. I told him that it probably couldn't work because I was leaving for America the following Tuesday and wanted to remain in Venice.

"How about just for the day?"

"It's possible."

"I can come pick you up. It's no problem."

"I'll call you to confirm."

"Have you seen *La sciagurata*?"

"No."

"Where have you been?"

"In Florence."

"With whom?"

"An old friend."

"Who?"

"It doesn't matter. Listen, Antonio. Can I call you back? I am in the middle of eating dinner with a friend."

"Who?"

"Valeria."

"Invite her to the villa, too."

"I will have to see."

"Call me soon."

"I will."

I told Valeria a little about Antonio and his villa. She said that he sounded a little like Don Quixote, and like quite a character, too. He is a pain but an honest and loving one, I told her. She still seemed interested in talking about him and the villa. Alitalia pilot, huh? Yes. Very smart.

We cleaned the dishes and Valeria looked over the paper I was writing for the Toronto conference. She wanted to help me with the Italian translation, which she said was about trumpets not trumpet players. "Thank you," I said appreciatively. We turned on the tube and watched an episode of *Friends*, which is on every night in Italy. They used to show a lot more American shows—now there are only a few, *ER* for example. Watching American TV in Italian made it all worthwhile. Usually I watch only daytime TV, the soaps: *All My Children* and Oprah. Oprah is uplifting, even though she has never done a show on homosexuals in all these years. Makes me wonder why. Gay and bi-sexual teens are much more likely to commit suicide than straight ones. Peer pressure and denial and fear of violence. *Friends* had some gender-bending innuendoes, but no alternative characters. But they weren't homophobic, at least.

We watched a little of an Italian variety show. If it hadn't been in Italian, I would have gotten ill. Sexism sells, and "T" and "A" sells the most. While in America men enjoy big breasts, in Italy men like long legs. I used to watch a lot of pornography when I was in my thirties. It filled up my idle time and vented my frustrations. Now it seemed sickening, and the truth is I have a partner and we don't have cable. We adore each other, even though our sex life has recently taken a turn for the worse. Even the six months in couple's therapy hasn't helped. I had pushed Barb away so many times, she stopped being interested. She is a sensitive lover, but tended to be bossy at times, telling me to move here and there, and touch here and there and stop and start. I felt inadequate and unartistic, just going through the motions.

I love Barb to the very core of my being, which is very different from any of my previous relationships, in which I felt lost and unsatisfied, cheated upon and devalued. Yippee. Things were going to change. I would go home and tell her how much she meant to me, and how important it was that we work things through. She isn't cheating on me. But we do have that cloud of her family hanging over me. They think that I'm stealing Barb away from the family. What do you do when you marry into a wacky family, or vice versa? I keep mine at a distance now, not even going home at Christmas. I recognize their chilliness and my own neediness and have started to become an adult. I looked into the mirror and made changes.

I looked into the mirror and kept my hair really long. If Giotto had a daughter, and he probably did, though no one has written about her (so what's new?), I would have looked like her. I feel it in my bones. We are related. Giotto went to Padua to paint the Scrovegni Chapel in 1304 and I went with him. He needed company and someone to cook for him. On Sunday's we took boat rides down the Brenta River to Venice. I refused to marry and lived with my friend Ilsa in my father's Florence apartment. We had hundreds of friends because we were generous and opinionated and honest. We entertained artists from all over Italy and I did people's astrological charts, which were of great interest. My father died when I was thirty-three, pretty late in those days, and my mother kept on living with her new boyfriend, the herb vendor. My friend stayed married, but her husband the banker traveled, so who cared much? Plus he had a boyfriend. You know those Florentines, they are all gay. In the Renaissance, there were so many gay men in Florence that laws were passed bringing in prostitutes to continue the race. Baths abound in Florence to this day. We lived a comfortable life, off my father's savings, and we were untouchable because of his fame.

I had always known that I did not appear back on this planet until the twentieth century, when I ended up in a concentration camp in Germany, in Dachau. I was of Polish descent, from the town of Lodz. I played the cello and was not particularly beautiful. My mother, a seamstress, and my father, a writer, got me the best music teacher in town, and I studied at the local school. My brother, Mo, liked math and studied little. We were taken away because my father was a local dissident, writing against the Nazis. In the camp, I played for the SS guards at night. My family died, one by one, of typhus and were cremated. I survived and ended up in Flushing, Queens, where I got married and died from a stroke. That's all I remember of my past lives. Maybe more would come to me, now that the ghosts could help me.

The TV show over, after a horrific performance by Miss Italia on bongo drums, we washed up and I told Valeria that I would give Barb a call at work—it would be short. Barb is usually busy with a client. She was starting a new firm and the stress was palpable. When Barb got stressed out, she would ask me to pick up my things around the house and get that crap, which had been sitting there for months, out of the refrigerator. Put some Klorox in the toilet, will ya? She suffered a lot from nerves, and used to numb them with pot. But not anymore. She is an adult. Maybe jogging would help. I loved her deeply and felt for her.

"May I help you

"Barb Hoffman, please."

"Is this Jean?"

"Yes."

"This is Amy. The receptionist. How is Italy?"

"Great."

"I'm glad."

Receptionists are so nice to partners.

"Sorry, Jean, Barb is on the phone."

"Can you tell her to call me tomorrow morning, my time? I don't want to interrupt."

"Sure. You take care now."

"Thanks, Amy."

Valeria was busy in the bathroom, washing up, when I saw Angela again. She was standing in the living room scowling at me. "What do you want?" I asked her.

"Nothing."

"Can I help you with anything?" I changed my tone to one of compassion.

"No. I am just as miserable now as before I took my life."

Honestly, Angela was starting to annoy me. When I went to the bathroom, I sensed her presence behind me. When I brushed my teeth, I sensed her peering over my shoulder. I started getting a little frightened. I walked to the kitchen, and she stood by the sink.

"Jean," Valeria said.

"Yes?"

"Do you mind if I read a little?"

"Not at all. I have something I need to finish out here," I

yelled back at her.

"Listen, Angela. Go on. Go live in your world. Let Valeria be. She is suffering enough."

"No."

"What do you mean, no?"

"No."

Trembling, I told her, "Get a life."

I picked up my cellphone and punched in Miriam's number. In a hushed voice, I said, "Miriam. A ghost is bugging me. She won't leave me alone."

"Find a candle and make a wish into the candle. Tell the ghost to leave you alone. I will help you from this end."

"OK, talk to you later."

I rummaged around the apartment for a candle and found nothing. I searched the drawers, the cabinets, the closet. Nothing. I sat down defeated, until I saw one right in front of my eyes on the desk where I was working. It was a green candle in a miniature clay flowerpot. It was for warding off mosquitos. This should do the trick. I found a match near the kitchen sink, lit the candle and put it on the desk. I stared into its scented, small flame and repeated three times, Go away, go away, go away. Three seemed to be the correct amount. Three, a perfect number in medieval numerology. Three, the beginning, middle, and end. Three, the times the Giants have won the Super Bowl.

Angela was gone. I went back into the bedroom, where Valeria was busy reading a book about Kant. I picked up *Garden of the Finzi-Contini*, and we read until our eyes were heavy and the sounds in the street subsided.

Chapter 10

The next day we bummed around Venice. It was a gorgeously warm and clear day for late October. Everyone was out, the locals with their stubby-legged dogs. Valeria told me about a famous Venetian proverb she had heard growing up : *Se si vol rider, bisogna discorar de merda*, which translates as roughly "If you want to laugh, you have to talk about shit." And we did. Not the pigeon version, but about this and that. We walked over the Rialto Bridge in the direction of San Marco. The gondolas and water taxis passed below.

"Valeria, have you ever been on a gondola?"

"No. That is for tourists."

"Like the Empire State Building. I have never been on it."

"I suppose."

"Let's do it. I have never been on one, and I can't imagine leaving Venice without a spin."

She hesitated. "It is something Americans do."

"It will be my treat. I insist. You were so kind to come up and visit."

"It's notoriously expensive. A rip-off, I would say."

I thought about how Peggy Guggenheim used to take her gondola from her palazzo on the Canal Grande and float to her next business appointment. Mozart was in Venice when he was eight. He must have taken one. Gosh, everybody has.

We walked up to two gondoliers who were chatting at the gondolier stand. They did not stop to acknowledge us, and we moved on. Not a good sign, we thought. Now I felt like a gambler at the slot machines in Vegas. We stopped at the

Palazzo Manin, at another gondolier stop. A handsome and pleasant gondolier came up to us after he noticed us milling about.

"Want a ride? Signorine?"

"How much does it cost and for how long?" I said in my unintentionally brusque New York manner.

"It's 150 euros for between twenty and thirty minutes."

"Oy. That's a lot. $160 for half an hour."

"If he goes that far," Valeria cautioned me.

I thought about it for twenty seconds and said, "Yes. Of course."

He smiled at his friends, and probably made a Venetian comment about how big my behind is. "That's a big one, huh, fellas," was how I imagined it. Then I stopped caring. He hopped into the boat and lent his hand to Valeria to get in. Then he helped me, though I certainly did not need any. He told us to find some suitable pillows to sit on, then he moved to the back of the boat and propelled himself from the sidewalk, and we began to move. Gondolas, which have been around for centuries, are an amazing feat of technology. They are long, narrow, and black, with long ends that twist up like a mustache. The gondolier positions himself on the back right edge of the boat and stands on a little mat with the single oar in his hand. He places one foot in front of the other. The back foot leans against a miniature pedestal, where the thrust of his weight begins in the heel and then rolls over onto the ball and toes of his feet. His whole body is working, and he presses forward. The young man began chatting with Valeria, as everyone does. He said that few Italians take rides and he was glad to be able to chat with a customer.

"I am visiting Venice with my American friend," she explained, clearly enjoying things so far.

"She looks it," he said in Italian.

"She speaks perfect Italian," Valeria warned him.

"I am sorry."

We approached our first bridge. The gondolier began to shout a warning to his fellow paddlers who might be coming around a blind corner. People standing on the bridge took pictures of us and yelled things like "Having a good time?" We smiled and I felt like a body in an operating room. The gondolier bent his head so as not to take the bridge in the nose. We moved to make our first left and encountered another boat coming our way. The gondoliers motioned to each other, and for some reason we went first, on the left-hand side. The gondolier pressed against the side of the dilapidated palazzo and we inched past the traffic. We hit a larger waterway, filled with water taxis.

The gondolier said that the taxis make him sick, that they pollute the air and the water, and that there were just too many of them. He said that the gondoliers were dying out, that the job was too strenuous. His father was a rower, as was his grandfather. He started when he was fourteen, as an apprentice for his dad. They make their own boats too, in the garage of their house in Mestre. He makes a decent living, and they have a union that is pretty powerful. But he was getting sick all the time. Pushing the boat takes a lot of energy; then you sweat and then you are wet just hanging around waiting for your next fare. He said that he was suffering from terrible neck aches that he attributed to the cold, especially the cold of the late fall, when it was also misty.

Valeria was entranced with the man, and I was happy because I had felt sorry that I made her do something cheesy for American tourists and she was actually enjoying it. He said that he had been paddling professionally for ten years, and that he was not married. Then he waved hello and yelled at a friend rowing by. A boat with an accordion player floated past us, filled to the brim with tourists. A man was singing "O sole mio," which Valeria said was really funny because it's a song from Naples. It has nothing to do with Venice. Ha, ha, ha—the two had a good laugh. Valeria said that she was from Modena, which is impressive because it is the heart of Italy— like our Midwest. It's the salt-of-the-earth Italy, except with much better food.

We floated toward the Grand Canal and saw the Rialto Bridge rise to our right. We had entered the highway. Boats rushed off on all sides, and people sang and screamed at each other. The gondolier told us some basic history about the palazzi around us. One was being restored by the Pucci family, and one was owned by an Italian bank. They all looked colorful and falling apart. The bottom floors were filled with water. Then he said a couple of words about the *forcola*, the wooden thing that holds the gondola paddle. With a subtle twist of the arm, he could make the boat go in any direction he wanted. He said that it had a unique design. It looked like a black Q-tip. Valeria listened in awe to what he had to say about its engineering genius, and the centuries it took to perfect. Strangers talk a little too long to Valeria. Once I heard a guy in Volterra explain the entire history of ice cream to her, from the Middle Ages to the present, claiming that his ice-cream place was the first to sell it to the public. I walked away, rude yet unencumbered.

We went about three hundred feet on the Grand Canal, until he made a dainty and precarious U-turn and we sloshed back to where we came from. By this time the gondolier was talking about how the Venetian government had stopped dredging the canals. No money, and no one seems to care about what happens to Venice. "They did more dredging during the Austro-Hungarian Empire than they do now," he contended. "The water stinks." Valeria nodded. "What is happening to Italy?"

He said that no one was in charge and that it should be divided up into little countries like it was in the nineteenth century. Valeria did not venture an opinion. She just bobbed lazily in the water. I fancied myself T.S. Eliot or Wagner, a famous artist floating in Venice. Every artist must have done this. It's like going to Disneyland if you love Mickey Mouse. Stravinsky is buried here. So is Ezra Pound. Peggy Guggenheim was buried in Venice next to her nine little white dogs, many of whom might have been called Fluffy, but I can't remember now. Venice has the power to transform the most stubborn and lost soul. No wonder artists and ghosts appear every so often. It's soothing. Besides the gondolier's crime of taking lots of my money for this short ride, there was no crime. I was not afraid to be stalked, attacked, robbed, road raged, school bombed, or mugged in Venice. We floated back to our original destination and Valeria had a huge smile on her face. Thank God. It was all worth it.

I paid the guy in my sabbatical lira and he helped Valeria and me out of the boat. He already had another customer by the time I was out. Business was booming this beautiful day. We saw another boatload of Japanese tourists happily find their places. Valeria said that she was thrilled and thank you, thank you, thank you. I told her that nothing could be of more value to me than her friendship. We walked toward the Biennale Art fair grounds. I had been there many years ago with her, and I wanted to revisit this fabulous, and the only grassy, part of the city. She hugged me around my waist and I noticed a tear flowing down on her cheek—then she said, "I want to buy you a book. It is about Elena Cornaro, the woman you are studying in Padua."

We walked into an unorganized Italian bookstore, and the

lady said that the title might be found up the stairs, to the right on a little balcony. We squeezed by her and found it on a shelf.

"It looks like a romance," Valeria admitted. "She has an affair with the noble Antonio della Scala."

Out the door, I asked Valeria if she had ever been with a woman. She said that when she was an adolescent, she had loved her best friend Perla. Together with their sisters they had played a knights and princesses game, when they would battle each other for the hand of the princess in their backyard. At the end Valeria (the knight) was obliged to kiss Perla (the princess), and she said that it felt beautiful. Valeria confessed that she was heartbroken when Perla found her first boyfriend. Their love for each other was over without a word. Soon Valeria found a boyfriend, and she embarked on the typical Italian love career, until she jumped ship and refused to get married. She dated married men.

Valeria stopped walking. "There is something I have been meaning to tell you for a while. I was too embarrassed."

"Please go ahead. You know that you can trust me."

"It's about Cesare."

"Please."

I suggested that we stop at a little café to talk. She agreed.

After ordering two sandwiches and Cokes, Valeria was ready to begin her story.

"Go ahead." I was really concerned.

"Remember two years ago, when you and Barb came to visit and you met Cesare and I told you that he was married and had a ten-year-old boy?"

"Yes. What about it?"

"A week after that, his wife interrogated him, wanting to know who he was seeing, and he told her the truth. He told her about me. He said that he needed both of his women, and hoped that she would understand. She just slumped in her chair and stopped talking for three days. She stopped eating. She stopped making sense. She demanded that Cesare stop seeing me. She followed Cesare one night and burst into my apartment, threatening to hurt me." She stopped. "She stopped going to work and ranted and raved. Cesare tried taking her to a doctor, but she refused." Valeria stopped. "Then she killed herself."

"Oh God."

"She doused herself with gasoline while sitting in her car and lit herself on fire. I wanted to tell you sooner, but I just couldn't."

I had only one thought: what is she still doing with Cesare?

"Cesare promises me that he doesn't have any other women, but he flirts with the woman down the block. He is a big flirt. But he had been very comforting to me, because he knows what it feels like to lose someone close to suicide. He talks a lot about his wife and says that nothing can stop a person from committing suicide once they have set their mind to it."

As much as this logic irritated me in this case, I said, "That seems to make sense."

The tale of suicide seemed to come full circle in Valeria's life. Her sister killed herself over her husband, her boyfriend's wife killed herself over his affair with her. Valeria was the common denominator. Was Valeria responsible in some way? Are people responsible for cheating on other people's partners? Did Valeria have a responsibility to be good to her sister and check in on her once in a while? Not for something as angry and vindictive as suicide. Suicide in the eyes of Valeria's sister was the ultimate revenge, like a stab in the heart. No one was responsible for this. In forgiveness, Valeria would find salvation from her pain. In forgiveness, I would embrace my embattled friend—alone, apart from her family, weighed down by an oppressive Italian society and her own feelings of inadequacy.

In listening to her story, I was made very aware of my limitations, of the vastness of experience and the journey I still had to make. Somehow, seeing Angela did not sit right with me, like a cold breeze on a hot summer day. Miriam understood. Dante too. But lately, I sensed that I was reading too much into my thoughts. Trying too hard to give feelings concrete meaning. Asking "Why? Why?" Imagining and making my feelings reality. But this reality needed to be understood over time to blossom. Italy had given me a stronger sense of self, and I thanked my companions on this journey, the mystics Miriam and Dante, my companion Barb, the exile Antonio, the seductresses Lisa and Paola, the artists Susanna and Dalu. In accepting my thoughts, I could grow. Not in deliberating, criticizing and rejecting. I know now: be true to yourself and just write. A new formulation of my reality.

The day came when I was to reenter the earth's atmosphere and return to Pennsylvania. I decided to take the local bus to the airport, since it would only cost five euros. I dragged my bags across the little bridges and dropped off extra clothes in a bin by the Piazzale Roma. The bus station was typical Italy. Confused tourists looked for ticket vendors who did not exist. There was no information booth in Piazzale Roma, as far as anyone could see, but when I asked a bus driver, who was smoking outside, he said to go across the street at the STA office. Who would know to do this?

I walked across the long piazza full of busses into a small, smoky office. The man behind a counter did not look up at me, for I was American. In my good Italian, I asked for a ticket to the Marco Polo Airport. He took my money, and I asked him where to get the bus. He pointed and said, "Over there where it says 'Mestre' on the sign." Demoralized and with ticket in hand, I waited for the bus with a few others, mostly young and wearing leather jackets. When the bus came, people filed on quietly, but as soon as they sat down, a symphony of cellphones commenced. Tunes from Beethoven's Fifth, Mozart's *Marriage of Figaro*, and Verdi's *Rigoletto* filled the bus corridor. Each person answered in a loud and distinct voice. In Italy, the louder, the better.

Table of Contents